"WE'RE BOTH ADULTS,"
SHE MUTTERED LOUD ENOUGH
FOR HIM TO HEAR. . . .

"As they say in the song," she added with a humorless twist, "it was just one of those things." She almost choked on the humiliating words. Unconsciously, she laced her fingers together. Despite the heat of the fire, she was trembling with cold.

And then her body jerked with alarm as she felt Spence's hands clasp her shoulders and spin her around to face him. "Are you saying our lovemaking meant nothing to you?" His eyes, which moments before had looked down at her with such passionate desire, were like green-flecked ice.

Claire's gaze dropped. "No," she mumbled. "It did mean something. But what could it have meant to you? You even called out another woman's name. . . ."

A CANDLELIGHT ECSTASY ROMANCE ®

154 A SEASON FOR LOVE, *Heather Graham*
155 LOVING ADVERSARIES, *Eileen Bryan*
156 KISS THE TEARS AWAY, *Anna Hudson*
157 WILDFIRE, *Cathie Linz*
158 DESIRE AND CONQUER, *Diane Dunaway*
159 A FLIGHT OF SPLENDOR, *Joellyn Carroll*
160 FOOL'S PARADISE, *Linda Vail*
161 A DANGEROUS HAVEN, *Shirley Hart*
162 VIDEO VIXEN, *Elaine Raco Chase*
163 BRIAN'S CAPTIVE, *Alexis Hill Jordan*
164 ILLUSIVE LOVER, *Jo Calloway*
165 A PASSIONATE VENTURE, *Julia Howard*
166 NO PROMISE GIVEN, *Donna Kimel Vitek*
167 BENEATH THE WILLOW TREE, *Emma Bennett*
168 CHAMPAGNE FLIGHT, *Prudence Martin*
169 INTERLUDE OF LOVE, *Beverly Sommers*
170 PROMISES IN THE NIGHT, *Jackie Black*
171 HOLD LOVE TIGHTLY, *Megan Lane*
172 ENDURING LOVE, *Tate McKenna*
173 RESTLESS WIND, *Margaret Dobson*
174 TEMPESTUOUS CHALLENGE, *Eleanor Woods*
175 TENDER TORMENT, *Harper McBride*
176 PASSIONATE DECEIVER, *Barbara Andrews*
177 QUIET WALKS THE TIGER, *Heather Graham*
178 A SUMMER'S EMBRACE, *Cathie Linz*
179 DESERT SPLENDOR, *Samantha Hughes*
180 LOST WITHOUT LOVE, *Elizabeth Raffel*
181 A TEMPTING STRANGER, *Lori Copeland*
182 DELICATE BALANCE, *Emily Elliott*
183 A NIGHT TO REMEMBER, *Shirley Hart*
184 DARK SURRENDER, *Diana Blayne*
185 TURN BACK THE DAWN, *Nell Kincaid*
186 GEMSTONE, *Bonnie Drake*
187 A TIME TO LOVE, *Jackie Black*
188 WINDSONG, *Jo Calloway*
189 LOVE'S MADNESS, *Sheila Paulos*
190 DESTINY'S TOUCH, *Dorothy Ann Bernard*
191 NO OTHER LOVE, *Alyssa Morgan*
192 THE DEDICATED MAN, *Lass Small*
193 MEMORY AND DESIRE, *Eileen Bryan*

RELUCTANT MERGER

Alexis Hill Jordan

A CANDLELIGHT ECSTASY ROMANCE ®

Published by
Dell Publishing Co., Inc.
1 Dag Hammarskjold Plaza
New York, New York 10017

Copyright © 1983 by Ruth Glick and Louise Titchener

All rights reserved. No part of this book may be
reproduced or transmitted in any form or by any
means, electronic or mechanical, including photocopying,
recording or by any information storage
and retrieval system, without the written permission
of the Publisher, except where permitted by law.

Dell ® TM 681510, Dell Publishing Co., Inc.

Candlelight Ecstasy Romance®, 1,203,540, is a registered
trademark of Dell Publishing Co., Inc.,
New York, New York.

ISBN: 0-440-17375-2

Printed in the United States of America
First printing—December 1983

To Our Readers:

We have been delighted with your enthusiastic response to Candlelight Ecstasy Romances®, and we thank you for the interest you have shown in this exciting series.

In the upcoming months we will continue to present the distinctive sensuous love stories you have come to expect only from Ecstasy. We look forward to bringing you many more books from your favorite authors and also the very finest work from new authors of contemporary romantic fiction.

As always, we are striving to present the unique, absorbing love stories that you enjoy most—books that are more than ordinary romance.

Your suggestions and comments are always welcome. Please write to us at the address below.

Sincerely,

The Editors
Candlelight Romances
1 Dag Hammarskjold Plaza
New York, New York 10017

CHAPTER ONE

Claire Tanager stood to the sound of applause. A bit self-conscious, she smoothed the skirt of her dark blue designer suit and then started up the long aisle toward the stage. Waiting for her with an air of eager anticipation was the president of the East Coast Association of Community Newspapers.

"Congratulations," the balding official boomed. With a flourish he handed over the brass and teak plaque with EMERSON MILLS GAZETTE engraved in flowing script across the front. Beneath the citations were the words BEST NEWS DEPARTMENT IN A CIRCULATION AREA OF UNDER 30,000.

Claire read the inscription with both pleasure and pride. This was the fifth award she had accepted during the afternoon's ceremonies and, as publisher, she felt a glow of accomplishment in knowing that two years of dedicated hard work had finally paid off.

Her blue eyes rose from the shield-shaped plaque, and she looked out over the audience with a smile that lit up her whole face. "I know it's customary to acknowledge everybody for their help in making a major award possible," she began. "But this time it's really true. There's no way I could be standing here without the support of a dedicated, competent, and hard-working staff. And I don't just mean the *Gazette*'s news department," she went on, her voice ringing with the overflow of emotions she felt. "Everyone, from our paste-up people and photographers to our news editor, Joe Vicchio, has a share in this recognition."

The editors and publishers broke out in applause again and Claire found herself grinning broadly now, all semblance of modesty having deserted her. This was a triumph she had worked hard for, and she was going to enjoy it to the fullest.

As her sparkling gaze surveyed the approving audience, her attention was briefly caught once more by a powerfully built man with a thick shock of curly brown hair. Several times during the day she'd found him looking at her with a speculative gleam in his deep hazel eyes. The invitation in that expression had been clear, but picking up a stranger at a two-day convention was just not Claire's style. Besides, he wasn't her type. She liked her men smooth and civilized. This character, who stood a head above most of the other men in the assembly and was built along Olympian lines, looked like he'd be more at home on a football field than in a press room. But despite her peremptory dismissal of him as potential romance material, at the moment she was high on success and, with sudden impishness, did not immediately avert her gaze from his. Instead, she looked directly into the rich forest-colored depths. The result was unexpected. A dart of electricity seemed to bridge the gap between them. For a moment Claire was almost disoriented, forgetting the rest of the audience and even the plaque her fingers now unconsciously clutched. But she recovered herself quickly. Tearing her captive gaze from his, Claire looked down at the red-carpeted steps. It was time to make a graceful exit from the podium, and she'd better watch her step. It wouldn't do to fall flat on her face, she told herself wryly.

Claire's big award was one of the afternoon's last. Back in her bright pink-and-red room an hour later, she gratefully kicked off her beige high-heeled sandals. After wiggling her toes luxuriously in the hot pink shag rug, she flopped onto the round waterbed that adorned her suite at the Ivy Bower Inn. With a sigh of pleasure she leaned back against the velvet tufted headboard with its ornate gold and white scrollwork that might have fit right into an old Theda Bara movie. And what would Theda have thought about the mirrored ceiling? she wondered. Giggling, she twisted her delicate features into a parody of a come-hither look and twirled a strand of dark hair suggestively as she gazed up at her reflected image spread out on the ridiculous bed.

Had the off-season rates persuaded the convention's committee to select this mountaintop honeymoon palace for their annual awards weekend? Or did one of them have a puckish sense of humor? she asked herself, looking up once more at her incongruous tailored businesslike reflection awash in the sea of pink and white quilted silk that must be standard issue at this aggressively opulent retreat for lovers. But in her present mood the overdone room only added to her good spirits. Sitting up, she reached for the white and gold phone on the French provincial bedside table and put through a long distance call to Joe Vicchio.

"Five awards," she exulted when his brisk voice greeted her at the other end of the line. "Even I wasn't counting on so many—including best news department," she added significantly.

Joe's whistle of pleasure said it all. Since her father's

death, she'd worked hard to turn a stagnant small town paper into a vital community force. And Joe had been right there by her side working the same long hours. She remembered the day the thin, intense young man with his deliberately dramatic handlebar mustache had come to her office. Fresh out of the University of Maryland journalism school, he had practically demanded a job. At first she had been put off by his brashness and his affected appearance. But it didn't take long to realize that hiring him had been a real stroke of luck.

"Tell the staff for me," she requested. "Or better yet, take them all over to your favorite hangout for a drink."

Always the pragmatist, Joe chuckled appreciatively. "That will be even better than hanging a plaque on my office wall. But what about you?"

The question triggered a spur-of-the-moment decision. After all, the tremendous effort she'd put forth deserved more than just a plaque too. "I think I'll take the weekend off," Claire told him. "See you on Monday, when we start on our next award-winning year."

"Right on!" Joe cheered. "And have a good time. You've earned it."

After she'd replaced the receiver, Claire pushed back a stray curl of dark hair from her high forehead and looked around her room again. The decor might be absurd, she mused, but the bathroom truly outdid itself. The walls were mirrored tile threaded with gold veins; the sink looked like a giant seashell; and the tub was heart-shaped and big enough for two.

What would it be like, she wondered, to spend a honeymoon here? She could just imagine Richard's reaction to all this tasteless tomfoolery. He had wanted to honeymoon in Paris, and if circumstances had been different, they would have made that trip long ago. A frown began to knit Claire's finely arched brows. Postponing their engagement hadn't been an easy decision two years ago, and the truth was, despite her success with the *Gazette,* she still had doubts about the direction her life had taken.

"Just until I get my father's paper back on its feet," she'd assured him at first. But those few months had stretched beyond the point that even she knew was reasonable. Of course the relationship with Richard hadn't ended, she assured herself. They still saw each other, and there had been an understanding that eventually they would find a way to work things out. But there had been something troubling about their last few meetings. When she tried to dredge up concrete evidence, there was nothing she could put her finger on. But somehow she'd sensed that he was drawing away from her. Finally, when she'd last met him in New York three months ago, he'd put some of his feelings into words.

"When are you going to get tired of playing Lois Lane Takes Over and come back to New York and to me where you belong?" he had demanded. Her reaction had been to hedge, because she didn't honestly know the answer herself.

"Better watch out! You just might lose me," he'd joked. His words had made Claire look up in alarm. But when their eyes met, his classically handsome features had molded themselves into a disarming smile that took the sting out of his warning.

From the day she had first come to work for him at *Style* magazine, Richard Buchanan had been able to charm her. And maybe he always would, she thought with a sudden sharp longing to hear the sound of his well-modulated voice.

And yet she felt just a hint of apprehension as she reached out once more for the elaborate rococo phone. Usually they made their dates well in advance. Suppose he had other plans for this weekend?

But, she reasoned, she was in Upstate New York already, and she had the weekend free. Why not spend it with Richard? Just then she heard his secretary's voice. "Mr. Buchanan's office."

"Hello, Miss Sellers. May I speak to Mr. Buchanan, please," Claire asked. "Tell him Ms. Tanager is calling," she added, believing that her name would put her through without delay.

There was a slight pause. "I'm sorry, Ms. Tanager. Didn't you know? Mr. Buchanan won't be available for another week. He's in Paris on his honeymoon."

Claire felt the blood begin to slowly drain out of her head. "Honeymoon?" she repeated stupidly.

"Yes. I assumed you knew. Mr. Buchanan was married a week ago."

The voice was as crisp and impersonal as a disaster list after a plane crash. And Claire felt as though she'd just plummeted to earth. A moment ago she'd been flying high on success, but now all the air had been knocked from her lungs.

"Can I take a message and have him call you?" the woman asked politely.

"No," Claire managed to get out through a mouth that felt dry as cotton before swiftly replacing the receiver. For several minutes she just sat limply on the edge of the bed, staring off into space while her shocked brain tried to make sense of the conversation. Surely it wasn't true! How could Richard have married so soon after their last meeting? She'd felt hints of something amiss, it was true. And then there had been his casual words of warning. But she hadn't expected anything like this. Who could he possibly have married? she questioned.

The surface of Claire's skin felt clammy. Suddenly lightheaded, she pressed an icy hand to her forehead. It must have been a whirlwind romance. Numbly, she pictured him in a variety of romantic settings with a woman other than herself. Had he taken her to all their special haunts and whispered the same passionate words? They were in Paris now, enjoying the honeymoon that might have been hers. And she had only herself to blame. Heedless of the damage to her makeup, Claire hid her face in her trembling hands. It had been her decision to go back home after her father died and take on the management of his paper. And now that decision was having repercussions she had not anticipated. At the time, she had told herself she was simply interested in saving the *Gazette*. But once she had become her own boss, she had discovered how much she liked that role. She hadn't wanted to give up being publisher of Emerson Mills's only paper. Now she could see that her determination to continue in a role she enjoyed so much had helped push Richard away.

Stumbling to her feet on legs that now felt rubbery, Claire made her way to the bathroom and bent down to run water in the enormous tub.

Soaking her troubles away had been a panacea since she was a child, and automatically she sought that refuge now. But as she shed her clothes and tested the steamy water, the heart-shaped tub and mirror-tiled walls that reflected back her slender, woebegone image only served to emphasize her troubles. She had taken Richard for granted, she acknowledged. And she could see that she had stretched their relationship too thin. Richard had understood what was happening, she realized with sudden insight as she remembered his gradual withdrawal. If he were really as important to her as she thought, wouldn't she have heeded his warning? she asked herself now. Why hadn't she done something to cement the bonds that held them together when she felt them beginning to crumble?

But Claire's muddled thoughts were too painful to dwell on. Wearily, she closed her clouded blue eyes and sank down into the soothing warmth of her bath. Deliberately making her mind a blank, she let herself drift in the comforting, liquid environment. But gradually the water cooled, and it was time to emerge and face reality once more.

Claire had never been one to wallow in self-pity, and now she made a valiant effort to pull herself together. She had planned to pamper herself this weekend. She knew there was a party for those conventioneers who'd stayed past the luncheon ceremonies. Briefly she considered going. But she didn't feel like accepting any more congratulations now—or making small talk. Perhaps a good dinner in the resort's baroque dining room would lift her spirits.

Decisively, Claire pulled out a rich blue blouse-and-skirt ensemble that brought out the color of her eyes. Its soft skirt complimented her tall, elegant figure. She had brought it because it never failed to make her feel attractive and feminine—and she certainly needed something like that now. To heighten the effect, she took a bit of care with her makeup, accenting her wide-set eyes with silvery blue shadow and brushing a soft pink blusher over her high cheekbones. Tall and almost too slim, Claire now looked elegant and patrician. It was the natural grace of her appearance that had first attracted Richard. But she wasn't going to think about him now.

However, once she reached the hotel's sumptuous lobby with its gold-flecked red wallpaper and composition marble statues of Venus and Adonis flanking each entry, her resolve wavered. Passing an enormous gold aviary in the central foyer, she eyed the roosting lovebirds with a shake of her head. They made a pretty picture, all right, until you looked down and noticed that their gilded cage had not been cleaned recently.

Turning on her heels, she marched across the terrazzo floor with its inlaid off-red hearts. There was a magazine rack in the little shop on the other side of the lobby, and she couldn't stop herself from heading for it. However, to get to the reading material, she had to wend her way through several counters loaded with the likes of flavored massage oils, aphrodisiac bath crystals, and inflatable bath pillows shaped like lips.

Ignoring the honeymoon how-to manuals, Claire reached for a *Newsweek*. As publisher of a slick fashion magazine with a huge national circulation, Richard Buchanan was important enough so that his recent marriage might rate a paragraph or two. And sure enough, when Claire's trembling fingers turned to the Life Style section, Richard was there smiling into the eyes of a petite blonde who gazed worshipfully up at him. The photograph dashed cold water on Claire's attempt to pretend she didn't care. And the brief paragraph beside the picture made it worse.

"Surprise wedding for one of New York's most eligible bachelors," it crowed. "Handsome and successful publisher, Richard Buchanan, and model-actress Susanna Billings have been an item for the past few months. But now the good-looking duo have made their alliance permanent. Susanna has given up her career for marriage. 'I only want to be a star for my husband,' the pert Mrs. Buchanan avowed as she and her new husband stepped on the plane for a romantic interlude in Paris."

"You want to buy that, lady?" the counterman asked, eyeing her curiously. Suddenly, Claire became aware that she had rolled the magazine backward, unconsciously digging her nail through the picture of Richard and rumpling the journal badly.

White-faced, she quickly drew a bill from her purse and paid the attendant. Then she shoved the magazine, still rolled to the Personality section, into the swinging lid of a trash bin against a nearby wall. Turning like an automaton, she reentered the lobby. In her distress she was so lost to the world around her that she didn't see the tall bear of a man who had been watching her intently ever since she'd stepped out of the elevator. His speculative hazel eyes followed her progress as she walked stiffly toward the dining room. When she had disappeared from view, he strolled over to the bin and extracted the still-protruding periodical. After noting the damage, he calmly scanned the article about a publisher's recent marriage, while the counterman looked on with mounting curiosity. When his customer finally finished and returned the periodical to the receptacle, the hotel employee grinned up at him knowingly.

"She's some good-looking lady," he observed. "But she sure has a strange way of reading a magazine."

The other man nodded. Pushing himself away from the counter with a solidly muscled arm, he sauntered out in the direction Claire had taken a few minutes before.

Once seated, Claire surveyed the hotel's restaurant under raised eyebrows. With its gold pilasters topped by entwined plaster hands, deeply tufted red velvet banquettes, and candlelit tables, it was, to her now disenchanted eye, as grotesquely romantic as the rest of the resort. There were even red satin swings dangling at intervals from the domed ceiling. And each was adorned with a soft sculpture cupid. Averting her gaze from one of these grinning cherubs, Claire snapped her heart-shaped cocktail list closed and ordered a stiff martini. She didn't usually drink very much, but tonight she needed something to blur her painful thoughts. While she sat sipping the potent cocktail, she skimmed the white and gold menu. It was just her luck, Claire told herself with grim humor, that she was having to cope with the end of a love affair in a setting designed for ecstatic honeymooners. Her mouth twisted self-derisively as she forced herself to focus on the flowing script offering such delicacies as Chicken Amoretto and Veal Venus.

It was while she was deliberating sardonically over Rack of Lamb Rapturous and Poulet Passionata that she heard a richly deep male voice observe, "It's a crime for a beautiful woman to eat alone in a setting like this. May I join you?"

Claire's automatic refusal died in her throat as she looked up and met again the intent, dark-flecked depths of the hazel eyes she'd encountered earlier. Again she was conscious of that bewildering stab of attraction. And combined with it, the feeling that her uninvited visitor was looking at her as though she were a lover he'd lost and then unexpectedly found. Why? she asked herself as her gaze traveled over the tall stranger who now stood next to her table. Slowly, she took in thick curly hair that framed a broad forehead. Heavy, dark brows formed straight barriers over his deep-set eyes. Under an assertively crooked nose, she noted a mouth that was both sensual and uncompromising. A cleft chin completed the arresting face. And below that remarkable physiognomy were tweed-covered shoulders so massive they seemed to stretch the limits of credibility. One muscular hand rested on the fluted pilaster next to Claire's table; the other was shoved casually into the pocket of dark wool slacks.

In different circumstances and in a more positive mood, she might have greeted his overture more kindly. Though he did not have the type of aristocratic looks she admired, he did radiate a male magnetism that was somehow very compelling. But at the moment she was definitely not feeling gracious. And his assumption that she wanted his company irritated her. Did she look like a woman who'd just been jilted?

"Nevertheless, dining alone is what I had in mind," she retorted, looking pointedly back down at her menu. But if she had expected him to take the broad hint and leave, she was mistaken. Instead of taking her cue, he pulled out the delicate gold and white chair opposite and settled his muscular bulk onto its spindly frame.

Startled, Claire looked up and studied the incongruous beachhead he had established. "Do you think that fragile chair is capable of supporting so much charm?" she challenged, unable to suppress the acerbic amusement in her voice.

He gave her back a calm smile. "I may look like the proverbial bull in the china shop, but actually I'm the soul of gentility. I treat delicate things with infinite care."

Claire stared in surprise. At first glance he might seem unpolished, but he certainly didn't sound that way. His deep voice was as smoothly assured as Richard's. Maybe she had been too quick to judge.

Before she could muster a reply he had summoned the

waiter, requested a menu, and ordered a Scotch on the rocks.

"This is quite a bill of fare," he remarked casually, surveying the whimsical list of entrees with a raised eyebrow.

"Well, since you weren't invited to partake, you needn't order," she pointed out silkily.

"Oh, I wouldn't miss the pleasure of discovery," he rejoined, neatly sidestepping her gibe. "I believe I'll have the Roulade of Beef Rendezvous. How about you? I'll bet the Peppered Tenderloin Divine is good. If you order that, we can have a bite of each other's."

Speechlessly, Claire stared at him for a moment and then deliberately laid her menu down on the table. "I don't know what you have in mind, but I certainly don't want a bite of anything that belongs to you. In fact, I'll pass on dinner and eat somewhere else," she clipped out, beginning to push herself off her chair. But his broad hand laid quickly on hers forestalled her exit.

"My apologies," he said earnestly. "I was out of line. I have a tendency to speak without thinking. The convention's over and we're both alone. I think we can have an enjoyable dinner together, and I promise not to speak again without thinking."

Claire eyed him warily, caught a little off-balance by the sincerity in his voice. "You're not exactly the shy type," she muttered, suppressing the unwilling admiration she was beginning to feel. Though in business dealings she'd learned to be chary of forceful men, the female in her couldn't help but respond to strength of will and purpose in a male. And this stranger clearly had those qualities in large amounts.

Her gibe seemed to roll off his massive frame like a

gentle rain off an impervious slate roof. He grinned for the first time, and Claire was almost shocked by the engaging softness it imparted to the granite contours of his face. "You're absolutely right; I'm not shy. When I see what I want, I go after it."

Again Claire was at a loss for words. To moisten her throat she took a healthy swallow of her drink. "Am I to take that as meaning you want me?" she questioned, struggling to keep her voice level.

Suddenly his expression was completely serious. "Oh, yes. From the first moment I saw you sipping the welcoming coffee two days ago, I decided I wanted to get as close to you as that cup."

For the second time Claire considered leaving, and for the second time his hand covered hers. "You've gone pale," he observed with concern. "Have I frightened you? Believe me, there's nothing to be alarmed about now. We're in a very public place." He gestured dryly at the large dining room surrounding them. It had begun to fill with couples, and a small combo was setting up next to the dance floor. "All I want now is to buy you dinner. Why don't we both just relax and let the evening unfold?"

His little speech aroused such a bewildering mixture of reactions that Claire found herself automatically reaching once more for her drink to give herself time to sort them out. Such a direct approach was flattering, of course, especially now that her ego needed bolstering. She had to admit that knowing this man wanted her was reassuring in the wake of Richard's devastating rejection. But at the same time she had no intention of following through with the game plan he was so clearly initiating. Yet, she had to admit she was intrigued and attracted.

What's more, maybe it was time for her to stop playing

the tragic queen in a Victorian melodrama. It was a role she wasn't enjoying very much. The man showed no sign of leaving her table, anyway, so why not let him stay? Truthfully, she didn't really want to eat alone. And, as he had pointed out, they were in a public place, after all. What could happen?

"I'm Spence McCabe," he interrupted her flurried chain of thoughts. "You needn't tell me your name. Claire Tanager picked up so many awards this afternoon that everyone at the convention has to know who she is."

Claire acknowledged the introduction with a slight inclination of her head. And, as if on cue, the waiter came over to take their orders. To accompany dinner Spence selected a wine which she recognized as unusually fine and expensive. The choice confirmed his earlier assurance that despite his rough-cut exterior he knew and recognized the better things in life. And indeed, now that she had the opportunity to study him closely, she could see that the white shirt opened at his deeply tanned throat was of the finest batiste and the jacket spanning his formidably solid shoulders was obviously custom tailored. He dressed every bit as well as Richard had, she admitted; it was just that he had the kind of build that would look more at home in a football uniform. An oyster shell Rolex watch stretched across the sinewy width of his hair-rough wrist, she noted absently as she watched his hand lift a delicate, long-stemmed water glass to his lips. And again she was struck by the incongruities he presented.

The waiter brought their salads, and Claire was glad for the opportunity to concentrate on something besides the overpowering man who had forced himself into her presence. But he would not allow her to ignore him. After only a few moments of silence he began to inquire about her background.

"How long have you been with the *Emerson Mills Gazette?*" he questioned. "You certainly don't look like a girl who comes from a circulation area of under thirty thousand." His eyes traveled admiringly over her glossy dark hair, finely etched features, and sophisticated evening blouse, lingering for just a second too long on the full bosom that was at odds with the rest of her tall slenderness.

Claire forced herself to return his look blandly. "Don't tell me you expect a small town girl to dress in gingham?" she inquired with false sweetness.

"Obviously not," he chuckled appreciatively. "But you haven't answered my other question. Does that mean you intend to turn the evening into a sparring match?"

Spearing a wedge of tomato onto her fork, Claire debated her response. Her less-than-friendly rejoinders to Spence McCabe were taking a lot of energy, especially after the martini she'd just downed. It would be a lot easier to do as he suggested, to simply relax and let the conversation flow more naturally. "In a way," she answered his question about her background, "I've been associated with the *Emerson Mills Gazette* all my life. It was my father's paper."

Spence pushed his own half-eaten salad away and leaned back in the delicate chair, causing it to creak ominously. "Well, you've obviously done a superb job with it. Don't tell me you learned everything you know hanging around the press room as a kid?"

Claire shook her head. "No. I got a degree in journalism from American University. And from there I went to New York where I worked for several magazines, including

Style." The name seemed to freeze on her tongue as she recalled her recent conversation with Richard's secretary. Spence watched her face carefully, his eyes narrowing as he took note of the grimace that momentarily shadowed her expression.

But just then the waiter arrived with the wine, and Spence focused his attention on the little ceremony that followed. After he had tasted and approved the vintage, the waiter filled their glasses with the ruby-red liquid. Claire took a tentative sip and then another. It was delicious and she smiled her approval. Whatever else one could say about Spence McCabe, he did have an appreciation of good wine.

Despite the ludicrous names on the menu, the meal that followed was quite good too. And Claire noted that Spence enjoyed his Roulade of Beef every bit as much as his beverage. But he was not too engrossed in his own dinner to neglect her wineglass. He kept it filled, and after the second glass, she lost count of how much she was drinking. *You'd better be careful,* one part of her mind warned. *But why,* another part answered recklessly. She deserved to relax and enjoy herself. After all, wasn't that what Richard would be doing right now? The image that thought conjured up made her reach for her glass and take another swallow. She looked up at that moment and found Spence watching her. The odd intensity in his expression jolted her slightly. Again she had the inexplicable feeling that he was seeing something in her she was unaware of. All during dinner he'd been pumping her for information about her background, she realized. And in her careless, feeling-sorry-for-herself mood, she'd given it freely. But though he now knew a great deal about her, she knew little or nothing about him. Part of her reluctance to ask questions was a stubborn unwillingness to give him any reason to think she was interested. But somehow all the wine she'd drunk had changed her perspective. It was silly, she decided a little fuzzily, to be so coy. After all, she *was* curious about him now.

"I'm tired of talking about myself," she threw out in a challenging tone. "What about you? You don't look like a newspaperman."

He smiled with dry humor. "I am though," he replied lazily. "I'm program chairman for the next Midwest small-paper convention. I'm here to pick up some ideas. And the setting your group has chosen certainly has got me thinking." He gestured significantly around the florid red, white, and gold dining room. It was now filled with starry-eyed honeymooners enjoying intimate dinners.

Claire couldn't suppress the bubbly giggle that escaped her as she nodded her agreement. "Well, don't blame me. I had nothing to do with picking this place."

The well-marked laugh lines around Spence's eyes began to crinkle. "Don't apologize; I'm enjoying it. All this makes a nice change from my usual routine."

"Which is?" Claire prompted, no longer trying to disguise her interest.

Spence toyed with the stem of his now empty wineglass. Their bottle had long since been drained and Claire was glad. There was no doubt that she was seeing the world through a pink fog.

"I publish a chain of medium-size papers in the Detroit area."

At any other time Claire would have reacted to this information with a diatribe on the evils of absentee newspaper management. As a small-town publisher with a keen and personal interest in her community, she believed strongly in on-site management. That was an important reason why she had left New York to live in Emerson after inheriting the *Gazette*. But in her present wine-induced mellowness, it didn't seem worth starting an argument over with a stranger. After all, she would probably never see this man again, and so what was the point? Instead, she let the conversation flow, surprised at the many topics that interested Spence McCabe and the depth of his insights into the real stories beyond many of the current news headlines.

"Well, enough profundities," Spence announced suddenly. "Would you like to dance?" As the evening advanced, the lights in the restaurant had gradually grown dimmer. But the darkest spot was the small dance floor, where a number of couples now swayed to the surprisingly pleasant selection of ballads being played by a mellifluous combo.

"Yes," Claire replied without hesitation. She'd always loved to dance and hadn't been able to keep from looking enviously at the slowly rotating couples now and again.

However, as Spence took her elbow to guide her toward the dimly lit dance area, she experienced a moment of doubt. His strong hand on the bare flesh of her arm sent little prickles along her nerve paths that were both exhilarating and alarming. And standing up next to him was a whole new experience. Claire was a tall woman, five feet eight in her stocking feet. She was accustomed to looking directly into the eyes of most of the men she knew. Even Richard had only been two inches taller. But next to Spence she suddenly felt tiny, delicate—and vulnerable! And once they gained the dance floor, the sensation was amplified a thousandfold when Spence took her in his arms. She was not so much dancing with the man as being enfolded by him. In her normally independent frame of mind, she might have resisted the overpowering sensation of being taken over. But tonight she was feeling weak; tonight she yielded to it, resting her cheek against his broad, tweed-covered shoulder with a small sigh of contentment.

Actually, despite his massive proportions, he was a good dancer—light on his feet and very agile. She had no trouble following his lead. It was just a matter of relaxing and letting him do all the work. And there was no doubt that she was quite relaxed now. She felt as though her bones were made of wax. Unconsciously, Claire molded her body to his, a part of her mind taking note of the male strength and power emanating from his giant frame. The solidity of his legs moving against hers through the softly draped silk of her skirt gave her a strange sense of well-being. And his large hand wandering delicately over her back, stroking and caressing her shoulder blades, was transporting her away. Gradually, as they moved in unison, following the slow, sensual rhythm of the love song the musicians were playing, it was as though she were lost with this man in a fantasy dream. Claire welcomed the escape. Around them on the dance floor the other couples swaying gently in each other's arms had become a misty blur. And the darkened lights of the dance floor were no more obscuring than the fog that had invaded Claire's brain. And right now she was more than ready to lose herself in a dream.

CHAPTER TWO

The combo played song after song, and the evening took on a heady bouquet like the wine Spence had ordered with dinner. The romantic music swirled in Claire's head, weaving a sensual pattern of half-realized desires. Unconsciously, she was clinging to Spence now, her breasts pressed against the hard wall of his broad chest.

He had leaned his cheek against the top of her head and his fingers were now curled around the delicate nape of her neck, threading themselves with sensitive precision in the dark strands of her hair. Her own hands had crept to his neck as well, where his wiry locks curled around her thumb, binding her even more closely to him.

Gradually most of the other couples left the floor. And when they were almost alone, Spence bent his head and whispered huskily in her ear, "Are you falling asleep on me?"

"Almost," she acknowledged. "All I need now is a glowing fire, another glass of wine, and perhaps a kitten on my lap." She giggled at the last request, wondering if Spence would understand.

But his response seemed to indicate that he did. "Well, I can't provide the kitten, but I can manage the wine and the fire," he told her.

She looked at him mystified, wondering what he meant. She hadn't seen a fireplace anywhere in the hotel. But he was already guiding her off the dance floor. To her surprise, after she collected her evening bag from the table, they exited the dining room through a side door and headed down a flagstone path away from the hotel.

"Where are we going?" she asked, her slightly tipsy brain beginning to react to the cool night air.

"To your fire, of course," Spence replied, taking off his jacket and throwing it protectively around her shoulders. The warmth in it from his body seemed to envelop her like a cocoon, and she willingly followed his lead as he turned down a side path.

Only a few moments later he was inserting a key into the door of a rustic cottage. "They have several of these surrounding the hotel," he explained as he ushered her inside. The room was dimly lit by a swag lamp in one corner. Claire could see two easy chairs and a long couch facing a fieldstone fireplace. The decor was definitely less obtrusive than at the hotel proper, Claire noted as she nestled down on the couch.

Although the setting was comfortable, doubts were beginning to flicker at the back of her mind. Perhaps she ought to be making an attempt to get back to her room. But Spence had already rolled up his shirt sleeves and was efficiently going about building a fire. She could hardly walk out on him now, when he had gone to such trouble at her whim.

When the flames had begun to flicker, casting long shadows around the dimly lit room, Spence disappeared through a door to her right. In a moment he was back, holding a chilled bottle of white wine and two long-stemmed glasses. "All the amenities," he informed her easily. She watched while he uncorked the bottle and handed her a glass. Like the wine he had ordered at dinner, this one was superb—although quite different in character. It was smooth as silk on the tongue and rolled effortlessly down her throat, starting up a little glow inside her that matched the one in the fireplace.

Claire leaned back against the soft cushions and sipped her wine slowly. She had an odd feeling of detachment, as though she were watching this scene in a movie or reading it in a book. For all of her twenty-eight years she had lived by a strict code of obligation and responsibility. But today's emotional highs and lows had somehow burned out her ability to make rational judgments. Tonight all she wanted was to relax and feel good for a change, to let what was going to happen unfold. And Spence in some ways was the perfect catalyst. Despite his imposing physical presence, she did not feel threatened by him anymore, merely curious and intrigued. And, she knew unerringly, that he had nothing to do with the day-to-day reality of her life. He had walked up to her table in the dining room just when she needed reassurance of her femininity. And he would walk away tomorrow just as easily. What might happen between them really didn't matter in the scheme of her life, she told herself with wine-clouded logic.

Spence sat down beside her on the couch and lifted his own glass to his lips. "Do you have everything you want?" he asked softly.

"For the moment," she agreed, leaning back and closing her eyes.

Spence set his wineglass down on the table beside the couch. Then he reached over and removed hers from her unresisting fingers. She felt the sofa cushions move as he shifted his weight. One arm circled her shoulder, and then she felt the warmth of his other hand spanning her waist.

"Well, I don't have everything I want but I'm getting close," he rumbled, his tone touched with humor. In the next moment he had drawn her into an embrace. She did not resist him; Claire was long past that point now. She merely waited with a quiescent curiosity to see what it would feel like to be held closely, in this intimate setting, in those oaklike arms, her face pressed against that broad chest. It felt wonderful, she soon discovered—comforting, reassuring, and then exciting. While his hands stroked the small of her back, sending a glowing warmth spreading past the fragile barrier of her silk blouse, his lips began to explore her face. He was a slow, unhurried lover. He did not immediately kiss her mouth. Instead, he caressed her forehead, her eyebrows, and closed eyelids; and then his tongue ran a gently erotic path around the outer coil of her ear. Claire waited with growing anticipation, wanting to know what his lips would feel like on hers. And yet she was incapable of initiating such a kiss. This was all unreal, a dream. She need only wait and let this pleasant, illusory interlude unfold.

Then his mouth settled over hers, gently exploring the relaxed line of her mouth, teasing her lips open so that he could invade the moist sweetness beyond. If the unaccustomed alcohol had dulled her senses earlier in the evening, the kiss was a potent antidote. Suddenly all of Claire's senses came quiveringly alive. She could taste the rich wine flavoring his breath, smell his clean masculine scent, and feel the slight roughness of his lean cheek as it came in contact with her own.

Involuntarily she sighed her pleasure. And Spence,

recognizing the acquiescence in the breathy sound, pressed her backward against the sofa cushions.

She felt his fingers gently stroking the path that his lips had followed over the contours of her face.

"I can't decide whether you're very close or far away," he murmured huskily, reaching up to curl a strand of her dark hair around his index finger.

"I'm nowhere real right now," she whispered back, looking up into the darkened depths of his hazel eyes.

A frown began to pull at his heavy brows. "Not real?" he questioned. "This is about as real as you can get."

Swiftly his lips descended to hers again. And this time his kiss demanded a response he had not asked for a few moments ago. The passion of the unspoken request opened the last barrier in Claire's mind. At first tentatively and then eagerly her own tongue met his in an intimate skirmish that made Spence sigh with satisfaction.

It was almost as if she had been wanting this man to make love to her for a long while, part of her mind acknowledged. And, at the same time, she had a strange feeling of recognition, as though his hands and lips already knew her body.

Shivering with delicious anticipation, she felt his weight shift so that his hand could find the buttons of her evening blouse. Claire closed her eyes as his fingers undid the silk-covered buttons and then slipped the sleek material from her shoulders. When he reached for the front closing of her bra, she shivered again.

"Claire, open your eyes and look at me," Spence whispered.

Obediently her blue eyes snapped open, and once more she was caught in the secret depths of his dark hazel stare. Still holding her gaze captive, he snapped the catch on the wispy bra and slipped that garment too from her shoulders. Spence barely touched her body during the whole operation. And that increased her anticipation to fever pitch. Slowly then, almost reverently, his hands came up to lift and cup her breasts. And it was as though he had kindled a fire in her veins. A moan escaped from her lips as his fingers began to caress their passion-sensitive skin. Her nipples ached for his touch, and she tried with her eyes to tell him what she wanted so desperately. But his caress had set its own slow, deliberate pattern. With the barest touch of his fingertips he began to trace delicate sensuous circles around her breasts, slowly—infinitely slowly—contracting the maddeningly erotic circlets.

It seemed to take forever for him to reach the throbbing peaks. And when he did, Claire gasped at the flood of sensuous pleasure that coursed downward through her body. Bending his head then, Spence repeated the fiery caresses with his lips and tongue. And Claire heard his own moan of pleasure.

Her senses were now tinglingly alive and tuned to this man. With possessive hands she reached up to entwine her fingers in his thick hair and cradle his head against her breast. When he lifted his lips to hers again it was with a new fervor that carried them both to a higher level of passion.

As Spence drew back they both gasped for air. His eyes smoldered with passion. And yet the hint of a grin played around the corners of his mouth.

"I'm afraid I'm a little too big for this sofa," he announced. "But the rug in front of the fireplace does look comfortable."

Wordlessly Claire nodded, her eyes drawn for a moment to the flickering flames before them. And then

Spence was on his feet, offering his hand to her. She let him help her up, grateful for the steadying touch. With deft fingers Spence removed her skirt and panties, and then angled his body away to strip off his own clothing. Watching him through passion-dilated eyes, she was struck by an image from her schooldays. Naked, he looked like the Greek god Atlas, who had been powerful enough to carry the whole world on his shoulders. When he turned back to Claire she had to fight to suppress a gasp. He was a big man—big all over.

As if reading her thoughts, he pulled her into his arms. "Don't worry," he whispered, his breath warm in her ear. "I won't hurt you. Remember, I know how to treat delicate things."

In the next instant he was lowering her body to the soft carpet in front of the crackling fire. Making himself comfortable beside her, he reached out to trace the outline of her swollen lips with one fingertip. Then he quickly pulled her into his arms again, pressing her pliant body against the length of his hard frame. The effect on them both was galvanizing. Claire arched her back to intensify the contact of their hips. And Spence began raining little electric kisses on her face, her neck, her shoulders. "It's been so long, and I need this so much," he murmured huskily into her ear. And fleetingly she wondered what he meant. But she was too caught up in the intensity of their mutual passion to ponder the words for long.

Then his lips were once again on her breasts, rousing their sensitive peaks anew. Claire sucked in her breath at the fire he was stirring in her body. The molten heat became even more intense as Spence's lips and hands began to weave an erotic pattern down her flanks and across her abdomen and thighs. Opening her legs, she began to rock her hips from side to side, unconsciously inviting even more intimate caresses. And Spence was glad to comply.

Claire's breath was coming in ragged little gasps now. Reaching down she entwined her fingers convulsively in the dark hair of his head. At her touch he raised his face, and she could see his need for her written in his impassioned gaze.

It was as though they were two strings of a musical instrument vibrating in concert. Spence did not have to ask if Claire was ready for him. And she did not have to urge that he complete their embrace.

True to his promise of gentleness, he entered her slowly, and yet there was a moment of pain and tension in which she couldn't help but draw back slightly. "Relax, love," he whispered into her ear, stroking her cheek with his fingertips. And she responded to the calming reassurance, letting him join with her completely.

He paused then for a moment, smiling down into her face with a tenderness that seemed to pierce her heart. But as he began to move she found herself buoyed up on a wave of passion. Eagerly her hips matched his rhythm as she gloried in the overwhelming feel of him inside her body. Up and up he carried her to the crest of the wave and then over the crest into a flood tide of sensation. Above her she heard Spence gasp his own shuddering pleasure.

Pale morning sunlight brought Claire gradually back to consciousness. For a long moment she lay in the unfamiliar bed, wondering exactly where she was and why her head was pounding so painfully. And then with a jolt her eyes flew wide open. Reflected in the mirrored ceiling was a scene that made her go cold with shock. There, like a tasteless tableau in a girlie magazine, was a rumpled, heart-shaped bed occupied by a naked man and woman. And she, with her dark hair tangled against the pillow and skin rosy with the glow of last night's . . . activities, was the woman.

Against her will, some of the scenes from the night before began to play themselves back through her memory, and she threw her arm in front of her face to try and banish them. But it did no good. She remembered vividly how Spence had made love to her in front of the crackling fire and then, when the embers had died, had carried her into the bedroom to renew their ardor.

Slowly, painfully, she turned her head to the side and stared in mounting horror at the sleeping form occupying the other side of the bed. It was a magnificently bare Spence McCabe. He was lying on his stomach, his face mercifully turned away from her. But the back of his thick curly hair was not what drew her attention. Instead she stared like one hypnotized at the broad expanse of his naked back and tapered line of his leanly muscled hips. Even under the circumstances, it was an impressive sight. And what's more, she admitted, her face growing hot, she knew the feel of those muscles intimately. Her eye was drawn to a set of scratches on his shoulder where her nails had raked a convulsive path during the height of their lovemaking. The memory made her face burn bright. Had she really been so carried away that she'd done something like that? She had made a fool of herself in the dark, and the last thing she wanted was to face Spence McCabe in the revealing light of morning.

Gingerly she sat up and then almost groaned aloud. Her head felt like a metronome gone berserk. But she was determined not to disturb the sleeping man. Stifling a moan of pain, she looked around the honeymooner's dream of a room, searching for her blue evening skirt and blouse. And then she remembered. They must be out in the living room, where Spence had taken them off the night before.

Grimacing, Claire slowly inched herself toward the side of the bed, vividly aware that she too was naked. What if he woke up while she was making her getaway?

But luckily the bed in this cottage had a conventional mattress which did not ripple and sway the way the waterbed in her room did.

With the greatest care she began to lever herself off the broad bed. But as her feet found the floor, Spence stirred, turning toward her in his sleep. "Kathleen," he muttered. His arm flopped over, grazing her naked hip, and she jumped up reflexively. But he did not awaken. And Claire had ample opportunity to study the expression on his slumbering face. What was he dreaming about? she wondered. Whose name had he called out? The man didn't even have the decency to dream about her, but was thinking of another woman altogether.

Self-disgust and then fury stiffened Claire's resolve to make a fast escape. She never wanted to see this man again as long as she lived. Turning her naked back on him, she stalked out of the room and closed the door quietly behind her, although the temptation to slam it was almost overwhelming.

The scene in the living room did nothing to assuage her feelings of humiliation. Empty wineglasses and clothes were strewn around the thick rug in front of the fireplace. And Claire gritted her teeth as she untangled her evening skirt from Spence's wool slacks. Her shoes were under a sofa cushion that had slipped to the rug. And her underwear was nowhere in sight. Afraid to take the time to look for it, she dressed as best she could, with an occasional nervous glance at the closed bedroom door. Finally, Claire grabbed her purse, jerked her wrinkled skirt straight, and fled.

Getting back to her room, even at this early hour, was embarrassing. Though few guests were about, several hotel employees gave her knowing looks as she did her best to cross the lobby with dignity and a bland expression.

Back in her own room she took a quick shower in a vain attempt to wash away her mixture of self-anger and chagrin. How could she have made such a complete fool of herself with a total stranger? she wondered. She might have gotten five awards for her paper yesterday, but Spence McCabe had certainly picked up the door prize.

Claire turned off the shower taps with a snap and then, with no consideration for her sensitive skin, roughly toweled herself dry. Within ten minutes she had dressed in tweed slacks, a silk blouse, and a tan corduroy blazer, thrown the rest of her clothes into a suitcase, and was heading out the door to pay her bill and leave. But as she stepped across the threshold, the phone on the bedside table jangled. Pausing, she eyed it doubtfully. It might be someone from the paper with a message. Or could it be Spence McCabe? The thought sent a cold shiver down her spine. Ignoring the phone, she shut the door firmly behind her and strode down the hall toward the elevator.

If the relentlessly romantic decor of the lobby had provided her with grim amusement the day before, it was now downright painful. Claire paid her bill as quickly as possible and then waited impatiently for her car to be brought up from the parking lot. But the foot she had been tapping restlessly on the pavement under the hotel marquee suddenly went still. Hurrying around the corner was a very large, very rumpled figure with a deeply preoccupied frown on his rough-hewn face. Claire slipped behind a large juniper next to the door and stood there trembling until she heard the glass door bang shut behind Spence. Surreptitiously she peeked out just in time to catch the eye of the uniformed parking lot attendant, who had driven her maroon Chevy Malibu up to the curb and was looking around perplexedly for its owner.

Feeling like a total fool, she emerged from the bushes, slapped a bill of unknown denomination into his hand, and slid into the driver's seat. With a sigh of relief she put the car into gear and pulled away from what she no longer regarded as a scene of triumph but one of personal disaster.

There was ample time for reflection on the long drive back to Maryland. Over and over again the scenes of the day and night before played through her mind like a video recorder with an endless tape. At first Claire was so distraught that she found it almost impossible to account for what she considered her bizarre behavior. She had always been scornful of women who engaged in one-night stands. And what else could you call what she had done? But, gradually, she began to find if not excuses then at least explanations for herself. She had been riding an emotional high before she had learned of Richard's marriage. The news had then sent her sliding downward like a tobogganist on an icy hill. And Spence McCabe had been there with open arms to catch her at the bottom. Realistically, she couldn't blame him for taking advantage of the opportunity fate had sent. Any man on the lookout for an easy conquest would have acted the same way. And she had certainly been easy.

The sound of a car horn made Claire jump, and reflexively her white-knuckled hand jerked the wheel. Her mind elsewhere, she had edged her car perilously close to the station wagon in the next lane.

Your little interlude with that man isn't worth getting killed over, Claire told herself pragmatically.

And there's no point in torturing yourself endlessly over a stupid mistake, she added. What was done was done. She must put this indiscretion behind her and get on with her life—which was publishing the *Emerson Mills Gazette.*

But as she pushed her car steadily south, her treacherous memory kept returning to the night before. Spence McCabe might have been an opportunist, and she had been ill-advised to succumb to his advances. But she had to admit that whatever else he had been he was a fantastic lover.

Yet it wasn't just that. She had thought herself in love with Richard. But Spence had wiped Richard from her mind like a teacher erasing yesterday's lessons from the blackboard. It wasn't only his lovemaking, she had to admit. There was more to it than that or even in her mood of rejection she never would have let him take her to bed. Actually, she had been determined not to even like him when he'd invited himself to her solitary dinner. But something about his warmth, his humor, and his compelling strength had affected her like a magic potion. If the truth be known, he had seduced her first with his personality and then with his body.

Yes, Spence McCabe was a man to be reckoned with. And once she allowed herself to think about him, she felt a welling heat begin to course through her veins.

CHAPTER THREE

That evening a rumpled and road-weary Claire turned off the major four-lane highway she had been following to the winding, wooded road that led into Emerson Mills. Named after an old flour mill hugging the banks of the Pawkata River, the town was a charming relic of a bygone era. Gray stone buildings lined the winding main street, which was nestled in the gorge the river had cut from ancient granite. Prosperity had come early to Emerson Mills when the Baltimore and Cincinnati stage line established a flourishing inn on the riverbank. Now the old stage stop was a museum which drew a steady stream of tourists to the historic area as did the rest of the town, with its charming boutiques, antique shops, and gourmet restaurants.

As Claire crossed the bridge spanning the broad, rock-strewn Pawkata at the foot of Main Street, she looked down with pleasure at the picturesque vista. Growing up in Emerson Mills meant that she had played on the riverbank as a child. And the music of its water rushing over the dark rocks was part of her. But there was another side to the river. Devastating floods were part of the town's history too. And though there hadn't been a major deluge in half a century, the high-water marks on some of the buildings near the bridge testified to the river's occasional destructive moods.

Just like mine, Claire thought as she drove her car up the winding main street and turned off on the side road that led to the Tanager family home. It was a three-story stone manor dating back to the antebellum period, and though Claire knew it was ridiculous to keep the house open for just one person, she couldn't bring herself to put the property on the market. She loved the old place, with its rich wood moldings, wide-planked oak floors, and plethora of rooms. And so many of her happiest memories were bound up in its stones and mortar.

As she pulled up the short gravel drive she could see the flickering electric candles gracing each of the house's hand-blown, double-hung windows. Keeping a candle burning in every window was a tradition her great-grandmother had started when a favorite son had gone off to fight in the Civil War. Somehow it had been continued through the generations. And Claire hadn't been able to give it up.

When she had come back after her father's death two years ago, her stepmother, Rose, had made sure the candles were still burning, just as they were burning now. Although she'd asked Rose to stay on in the house with her after Dad died, Rose had shaken her small blond head. "I never really felt I belonged here, Claire," she demurred. "And I think the best thing now would be to move. My sister in Florida has asked me to come down there, and I've written her to say I'm on the way." Rose's words had disturbed Claire. She could not deny the truth of her statement. Claire's father had been deeply in love with his first wife—her real mother. And when he'd finally remarried it was because of loneliness rather than any overwhelming passion. Although Rose had tried hard to fit in, Claire had remained far more important in her father's emotional life than Rose had ever managed to be. She had always felt some guilt over that. But it was too late to change the past.

Slowly Claire eased her car to a stop at the side of the circular drive and sat for a moment gazing up at the flickering candles. She couldn't help but compare this homecoming with that other one two years ago. Then she had told herself her stay would be only temporary. Now she knew it was permanent. In a way the decision had been made for her yesterday afternoon when she learned that she and Richard would never marry and make a life together. But if she were honest with herself, she would have to admit that the decision had really been hers, not Richard's. If she had wanted to be his wife, she would have turned over management of the *Gazette* to Joe Vicchio months ago and returned to New York. But she hadn't done that. And now she understood why. Her real commitment was not to Richard; it was to her family's paper and to the town where she had grown up.

What she hadn't come to grips with in the past, and what she now had to acknowledge, was the effect on her personal life. She knew and had dated most of the eligible men in Emerson Mills. None of them really attracted her.

As she looked up at the lights in the window, her eyes misted over slightly. Like most girls, she'd assumed that one day she'd have a happy and fulfilling marriage.

Unconsciously she shook her head and clenched her fists. It wasn't likely that would ever happen now. Suddenly, like driftwood caught in a strong current, her thoughts were pulled back to her night with Spence McCabe. With a little distance between her and the experience, she was able to admit just how much she had enjoyed first his company and then his lovemaking. She could acknowledge that. But she couldn't come to grips with how much the experience had affected her emotionally as well. Be that as it may, this was the first and last time she would ever do anything so impulsive. And in a way it was a fitting end to a stage of her life.

"But don't punish yourself for it, Claire," she whispered aloud. And then she added silently, *It was your first such indiscretion, and it will surely be your last.*

Slowly Claire opened her fingers and let go, just as she was now letting go of some of the romantic hopes and fantasies she had cherished since girlhood.

Back to business, she told herself sternly. *If you're going to make your mark in life, it's going to be as the publisher of the* Emerson Mills Gazette.

And with that she opened the car door, swung her legs out, and headed for the wide stone steps of Tanager Hall.

Claire had always used hard work to push aside personal problems. After the joyful victory welcome by her staff, she plunged into her job with what she could wryly see was the determination of an overladen locomotive going uphill on full throttle. Never content to be a mere figurehead, Claire had always taken an active interest in the *Gazette,* writing a weekly editorial, meeting with local businessmen on issues of interest to the community, overseeing the news and feature department, and sometimes even making final selections on photographs to illustrate stories. Her own journalistic background fitted her well to do this, and she was able to be a help rather than a hindrance to her carefully handpicked department heads. Now she redoubled her efforts, and six weeks later, as she sat back with the latest issue, she could tell that her labor counted for something. The paper looked better than ever. The articles were meaty, telling, and to the point, and advertising revenues had jumped in a way that was extremely satisfying.

But to her surprise, when she said as much to Joe Vicchio after their weekly staff meeting, his response was guarded.

"Sure, Claire, it looks good," he acknowledged, pushing back a lock of the longish black hair that had a way of slipping over his forehead. "But it *has* to look good—it's not as though we don't have any competition."

Claire glanced up questioningly. "Listen, Joe, if you mean *The Newton Voice,* I don't consider them our competition." As she spoke, Claire's patrician face had taken on an unconscious expression of hauteur. As the last surviving member of one of the area's oldest families, she could not help resenting Newton. The pipedream of an internationally famous developer, it was a planned city located fifteen miles from Emerson Mills. The instant community had mushroomed overnight in the rolling fields of what had been a strictly rural county. Though long-time residents had refused to believe the experiment would be anything but a failure, the city had quickly attracted people from nearby metropolitan areas. Along with money and a new business base, they brought with them urban problems that Claire and many of her readers felt threatened the traditional rural character of the region. And, like the brash young city, *The Newton Voice,* its recently founded newspaper, seemed an affront to the time-honored ways of the county on which it had intruded.

Ignoring Claire's dismissive look, Joe reached into his

briefcase and fished out a copy of the rival paper. "I know you think the *Voice* is a rag, but you ought to take a close look at it every week. We've been working hard, but so have they." He opened it to an inside page and gestured to a feature on a new Main Street business in Emerson Mills. "This should be in our paper, not theirs," he commented tersely. "And look at this piece on drugs and the county's teenagers. They scooped us on that one too."

A tiny frown began to knit Claire's fine eyebrows. Joe was right. And, despite herself, she was impressed by the look of the *Voice*'s layout.

"They've given Bruce Bramen, who went to the University of Maryland with me by the way, a free hand with the design. And Joyce Rushing is going after the features with a vengeance. If she doesn't pick up an award at that convention of yours next year, I'll be surprised."

Claire silently began to flip through the pages of the rival publication. There was no denying that Joe had a point. But she wasn't prepared for his next remark.

"Listen, Claire," he began, leaning forward and propping one bony elbow up on the edge of her desk. "You know that Bruce, Joyce, and I aren't averse to an occasional get-together for a drink and some gossip at Ethan's Tavern."

Claire smiled, picturing Joe as she'd never seen him before. He was always so brisk and professional around the office. But, like everyone else, he must have his human moments. Apparently he liked to get together with his cronies, drink beer, and gossip at Ethan's. And certainly there was nothing wrong with that.

"My feelings about the *Voice* don't extend to quarantining my staff members," she assured him. "Of course I know you like to have a drink with your friends." She leaned forward and patted his shoulder with mock motherliness. "It's okay, Joe. In fact, I wish you'd invite me along sometime. I'd like to meet my opposition, if that's what they are."

Her editor grinned. "Friendly opposition let's call them. And, in fact, they've passed along some very interesting information. It seems an outside syndicate called SJM Enterprises has just made the publisher of the *Voice* a very attractive offer and will soon be doing the same to you. It's just possible the *Voice* and the *Gazette* could be part of the same chain sometime in the near future."

Claire stared at her news editor in astonishment, all her instincts for self-preservation suddenly brought to the fore. "Never," she clipped out. "The *Gazette* and the *Voice* will never be part of the same chain—not if I can help it anyway. You know how I feel about chains for towns like ours. Emerson deserves to have its own independent newspaper, a paper where the local management really cares about the community. With a chain you don't have a local paper anymore. All you have is a mechanism for selling ads—with a few insipid news and feature stories thrown in so the people will keep turning the pages."

Joe threw up his shirt-sleeved arms in mock surrender. "Okay, okay. I've heard this diatribe before. I know how you feel. I'm not advocating that you sell out. I'm just warning you what to expect."

Claire pushed back the old wooden swivel chair that she'd inherited from her father and stood up. Her rust silk blouse was clinging to her back, and she rolled her shoulder in a stretching motion to loosen it. After a cold snap that sent her searching the cedar closet in the attic for her woolens, the weather had turned hot again. And though the wide double-hung windows in the mill building that her father had converted to a newspaper plant were open, her second-floor office was uncomfortably stuffy. She walked to one of the windows and looked out at the river lined on the opposite side with tall trees just beginning to show their autumn foliage. "I'm sorry, Joe." She turned and offered an apology and the warm smile that never failed to transform her face. "I know I can be pretty tiresome when I get on one of my favorite hobby horses."

The young man nodded. "No offense taken."

Claire looked him steadily in the eye, her smile beginning to tease now. "And you haven't said everything you intend to on the subject either."

Joe raised his hands, palm upward, in a gesture of capitulation. "All right, you've got me," he admitted. "I do have more to say."

Claire returned to her chair, folded her arms across her chest, and leaned back with exaggerated patience. "Go ahead—I'm all ears."

"I know you have definite ideas about local journalism," he began. "But you do have to face the realities of the situation. Emerson Mills isn't some isolated community in the middle of the Maine woods. Your circulation area overlaps Newton's. You know yourself that our ad staff spends almost as much time in the Newton Mall as it does on Main Street here in town. We raid their advertising sources. So it isn't surprising that they should go after ours."

"So what's your point?" Claire interjected. "You know very well we need that advertising in today's economy."

"That's exactly my point. If a syndicate takes over the *Voice,* you can bet it will be backed with money. If they can't buy you, they'll compete with you. They know as well as you do that it's advertising money, not subscriptions, that really pays the salaries at a small paper."

Claire gave him a questioning look. "And where is all this leading?" she prompted.

"Well, with outside money for backing, they can afford to undercut your advertising rates," Joe went on. "And they can also afford to wait around until you begin to weaken. So I'm just warning you, Claire. You can turn your nose up at this syndicate. But if you do, you may be in for a siege."

The scenario Joe had outlined was something Claire had never considered. Neither the *Gazette* nor the *Voice* had ever had the resources for the type of all-out war he was suggesting. But outside money could make a big difference. And so his words of warning lingered in her mind all week.

They were still threading through her thoughts as she drove back home the next Friday to shower and change for one of her infrequent dinner dates. Her escort for the evening was an old friend, Phil Carpenter. The county's assistant state's attorney, he had been divorced a few years ago. He and Claire had an agreeable but unexciting relationship.

As she stepped into the cool central hall, she could smell the scents of lemon polish and pine oil cleaner. Mandy was just finishing one of her twice-weekly attacks on faint traces of dirt and dust that accumulated on her days off. A moment later the cheerful middle-aged woman bustled into the hall, folding a light sweater over her arm.

"There you are," she greeted Claire. "You just missed a call from Joe Vicchio. He says 'the other shoe has dropped,' whatever that means."

Claire arched one elegant eyebrow. She didn't know

exactly what that meant either, but she had a suspicion it might refer to their conversation earlier that week. When she tried to return Joe's call, however, he wasn't in the office. And as she hung up the phone, it was with a feeling of tension. *Whatever's going to happen,* she thought, *I want to know so I can start preparing for it.* Joe's call was on her mind while she showered and changed into a soft lavender knit dress that modestly covered her arms and throat but flattered her high breasts and narrow waist.

Phil Carpenter smiled appreciatively when he picked her up a half hour later. "It does my staid reputation good to be seen with you, Claire," he remarked as he escorted her to the maroon Mercedes parked next to the ancient boxwood lining her drive.

Claire returned the smile a bit ruefully. She had never thought of Phil as anything but a friend, and she couldn't help reflecting how impossible it would be to have the kind of blazing sensual experience with this decorous male that she'd shared with Spence McCabe. In fact, if Phil had any idea what had happened at that ridiculous hotel in New York, he would probably go white with shock. Despite herself, the thought brought a grin to her face, which she quickly pressed back.

What kind of crazy line were her thoughts taking? she asked herself. Someone like Phil, not Spence McCabe, was the perfect companion for an unattached newspaper publisher living in a small town. It would be suicide to her reputation in a place like Emerson Mills to have anything but the most correct and proper dealings with the men she infrequently dated. She'd resigned herself to that fact long ago.

The charming country inn that Phil had selected for dinner was one of her favorites. And Claire had always found Phil good company. But though she made a valiant effort to listen to his small talk about doings at the county courthouse, her mind kept wandering that evening. Joe's pronouncement about the coming takeover attempt, and his mysterious phone call, had really unsettled her, she realized as she sipped her white wine and tried to relax. Yet she did make an effort to respond to Phil's conversation and even came up with a few amusing stories of her own. She knew everyone in town and was often the first to hear what was going on in a wide range of areas.

"Had you heard the Army Corps of Engineers is considering a flood control study of the Pawkata?" she asked.

"Considering?" Phil responded. "They should do more than consider it. The fact that we haven't had a major deluge in years doesn't mean it can't happen again. And, in fact, you know I worry about you down there at the old mill next to the river."

Claire grinned. "Actually it's a perfect spot. The editorial staff could always climb to the roof if there's any problem. But," she added more seriously, "you're right. It could ruin some of my father's old files in the basement. Some of those papers are invaluable. And when I get the chance, I'm going to move them upstairs."

The subject of disasters led Phil off into a story about a farmer who had burned down his own barn and tried to collect on the insurance he had taken out with two different companies. Claire nodded and smiled at the appropriate moments. It was amazing, she thought, how easy it was to conduct a conversation with most men. All you had to do was listen with a fascinated air and they went away praising you to the skies for your wit.

It hadn't been that way with either Richard or Spence McCabe, she thought, letting her mind skirt dangerous territory for a moment again before firmly drawing back from those two ill-fated episodes in her life. And the mental avoidance maneuver wasn't difficult to accomplish. Because the problem Joe had made her aware of was at the moment far more pressing. She couldn't help burning with curiosity to find out what his call had meant. And so it was with relief that when Phil dropped her off at the door with an undemanding kiss she was able to go inside at once and head for the phone.

It was before eleven o'clock. And she knew Joe would still be up. In fact, when he picked up the phone after only two rings, his first words were "Hello, Claire."

"How did you know it was me?" she questioned.

"I knew you wouldn't rest until you found out what my message was about. What took so long?"

Claire looked down at the receiver with a faint frown and then shifted it to the other ear. Usually Joe's teasing amused her, but sometimes she found it a little annoying. She was feeling needle pricks of impatience now. But that was probably because she had worked herself up to a fever pitch of apprehensive curiosity. "I was out for the evening. But I got back as soon as I could because I was going crazy thinking about your message," she returned. "So what's it all about? What other shoe has dropped?"

Sensing her mood, Joe abandoned his patronizing banter and launched into a succinct explanation. "After you left this afternoon I received a call from the general manager of SJM Enterprises. You remember who they are I'm sure."

"Yes," Claire returned tensely.

"They've come to an agreement with the *Voice* and would like to set up a meeting with you."

Claire made a derisive sound in her throat. "You were

right, Joe. They're fast workers. Well, I have no wish to meet with them."

There was a brief pause, and Claire could imagine the exasperated expression on Joe's dark narrow face. He would try to persuade her differently, she knew. And so it came as no surprise when he said, "I think you'd better not snub them at this stage, Claire. After all, remember the old saw 'Know thine enemy.' This is a good opportunity to do just that."

Claire took a deep breath while she paused to think. Joe was right. It would be stupid not to size up the opposition. "You win," she conceded. "When do they want to meet?"

Joe heaved a small sigh. "They're trying to come on like gentlemen. They've asked to get together sometime next week at a private dining room at Chez Odette." Joe chuckled. "I have to credit their research department. They know what your tastes are. At least we'll get a good meal out of this. I'm invited too."

Claire ran a slim hand through her short dark hair. "Well, that's good. You can lend me moral support. And, by the way, will I be meeting with the general manager?"

Joe's answer came over the phone in strong, clear tones. "Yes, we'll be meeting with Chris Graffenberg, the general manager. And the big honcho himself, SJM's president, will be along. His name is Spencer C. McCabe."

There was a long, frozen silence while Claire took the receiver from her ear again and stared at it. "What did you say?" she whispered, lowering her head to the mouthpiece.

Joe sounded puzzled. It wasn't like Claire to miss a message the first time it was given. "I said you'll be meeting with Chris Graffenberg, SJM's general manager, and Spencer McCabe, the president."

Claire flattened the palm of her hand over her suddenly

clammy forehead. "Thank you. I'll see you tomorrow, Joe," she managed to croak into the phone before hanging it up very carefully. She had just begun to put the pieces of her life together in a neat pattern. But suddenly, as her blue eyes gazed unseeingly at the now quiet phone, she had the feeling they were about to fly apart in a million directions.

CHAPTER FOUR

Even though Claire had agreed to the meeting, it took several rounds of inner debate before she could actually force herself to pick a date for the confrontation. But finally she told Joe to set up the meeting for the following Wednesday. The date reflected her growing qualms. For years now she'd thought of Wednesday as her lucky day. From winning her first spelling bee in the fifth grade to landing her first editorial position in New York, good things had always seemed to happen in the middle of the week, and whenever she felt insecure about a project she would try to tackle it on a Wednesday.

But after settling on the date for her fateful encounter with Spence, Claire chided herself for foolishness. Obviously, her luck had already run out. How could the meeting be anything but a disaster? she wondered as she flipped irresolutely through her closet, looking for the right outfit to wear. At best, she would be merely embarrassed by encountering a man who obviously thought of her as a pushover. But, at worst, the luncheon could be both humiliating and threatening.

If Spence McCabe was really serious about taking over the small newspapers in the area to establish an East Coast chain, he would probably use every available means of beating his opposition into submission. And what better weapon to wield against a female competitor, Claire asked herself bleakly, than having made a one-night stand of her only a few weeks earlier? But surely the man wouldn't sink so low. Though her experience had been so brief, he hadn't struck her as the mean or petty type. Far from it. Though what had happened between them hadn't exactly gone according to the etiquette books, nevertheless, Spence had been all consideration. You could tell a lot about a man by the way he made love, she argued inwardly. And in that department Spence had held back until he was sure of her pleasure before taking his own. In bed he had been the perfect gentleman. Hopefully he would continue, at least outwardly, to play that role.

Claire paused, staring down at the blue material she now unconsciously clutched in her hand. It was the outfit she'd worn that night. *If only I'd been the perfect lady,* she thought, *I wouldn't be in this fix now.* But instead of behaving with her usual decorum, she'd lost control and behaved like a fool. Furious with herself all over again, Claire extracted outfit after outfit, glanced at them with a frown, and then discarded them on the bed. Nothing she held up in front of the cheval mirror looked right now. She finally decided on dropping the blue outfit that reminded her of that night. Touching the fragile, yielding fabric conjured up too many memories she wanted to banish from her thoughts altogether. How could she possibly confront the man as a business rival when she was still thinking of him as a devastatingly potent lover? And if she was remembering him that way, how would he be thinking of her? The question made her stiffen. Claire's soft mouth set defensively. She had behaved like a wanton that night, letting herself be swept away on a tide of passion. To deny that memory, both to herself and Spence McCabe, the image she projected at lunch had to be as cool and professional as possible.

Finally she settled on a tailored navy blue wool suit and a print blouse that coordinated with her burgundy leather briefcase and pumps. The carefully chosen outfit made her look both sensible and businesslike. And when she pulled into the long drive leading to Chez Odette, she was feeling confident and in control.

Odette's was a historic mansion that had been converted into a restaurant more than three decades earlier. Its several rooms decorated in period fabrics and furnishings had both elegance and charm. And its menu, though limited, was excellent. It was the perfect choice for the meeting Spence had set up, and Claire knew that he must have done some scouting around before selecting it. Apparently he was a man who didn't leave details to chance, and she had to respect that.

When she and Joe gave their names to the maître d', they were guided to a small room off the main dining area that opened onto a terrace overlooking the river below. It was a charming setting but as Claire crossed the threshold with Joe Vicchio at her side, her eyes were riveted to the commanding presence of Spence McCabe. He was already seated at a table facing her across the small chamber. There was another man to his right, presumably the Chris Graffenberg mentioned in the letter that had prepared the way for these negotiations. But Claire was too busy drinking in the sight of Spence to spare much attention for his companion. He looked different, and all at once it came to Claire that he had probably dressed as carefully for this occasion as had she.

His immaculately tailored suit of charcoal gray wool fit his broad shoulders like a glove, emphasizing rather than disguising his remarkable physique. Certainly he looked considerably less ruffled than he had the last time she'd seen him. His hair had been recently cut, she judged. Its chestnut brown thickness was neatly brushed over his forehead, and as he moved his strongly molded head, the sunlight spilling in over the table from the window picked out sparks of red and gold.

All in all, he looked like what she now knew him to be—a very successful businessman, shrewd, determined, and accustomed to command. And as his hazel eyes rose to intercept her assessing gaze, she felt another little shock of recognition. This was the man who had captivated her with the force of his personality and then made thrilling and unforgettable love to her. And now, despite everything, she experienced a fierce surge of pleasure at the sight of him. Even though the situation she found herself in was intolerable, her traitorous feminine heart was glad that he was here—glad that, after all, it was not yet over between them. The realization flared across her consciousness like a searchlight and then was pushed resolutely back. Her blue gaze met the green-flecked depths of his and recognized the masculine challenge in it. As though a gauntlet had been thrown down and then taken up, Claire strode briskly across the polished planked floor toward the window-lit table where Spence waited. She was conscious of his eyes on her, the expression on his craggy face carefully neutral as he steadily tracked her approach. Yet she knew instinctively that her own careful sartorial preparations hadn't fooled him one bit and that he was remembering their last encounter as vividly as she.

When she and Joe were within a few feet, Spence got up,

his powerful body towering over Joe's slighter form, and held out a strong brown hand. "Miss Tanager, Claire, I can't tell you how much I've been looking forward to meeting you again." He turned to his associate, a short balding man somewhere in his early thirties. "And this is Chris Graffenberg, my marketing director." "Pleased to meet you," the man said, holding out a hand. "I've heard a lot about you, Miss Tanager."

Claire blinked. That was a shock. It had not occurred to her that Spence might have talked about her to anyone. She looked at him, her eyes beginning to dilate. Ignoring the accusation in her face, the big man turned to her colleague and said smoothly, "This must be Joe Vicchio. Claire told me she had a very superior news editor."

Joe swiveled and he stared at Claire, an understandably astonished expression on his mobile features. "You and Mr. McCabe have already met? Why didn't you tell me?"

Claire felt her neck go hot, and she could not stop herself from shooting Spence an angry glance. She'd been too optimistic in judging him a gentleman. Surely a gentleman would have refrained from mentioning their previous meeting and spared her the embarrassment of trying to explain it. But clearly that was not the game he intended to play.

"Mr. McCabe and I were introduced at the small newspaper convention I attended last month," she told Joe. "I had no idea then that we would be meeting again so soon."

"Life's full of little surprises," Spence agreed equably as he pulled out a chair for her on his left.

"Isn't it, though," Claire muttered between her teeth, accepting the proffered seat. When their drinks and their meals had been ordered, Spence leaned back lazily and surveyed Claire's faintly flushed face. "You're looking well, Miss Tanager, and your town more than lives up to the glowing description you gave me a few weeks back." He gestured expansively at the scene that lay spread before them out the window. Like a dreaming thread of silvered green, the Pawkata flowed between trees brightened by red and gold autumn foliage.

"I was telling Chris, before you arrived, that it was partly your description of the charms of this area that made me consider it seriously as a possible locale for investment."

Claire felt rather than saw Joe level an interrogative stare in her direction. Her own gaze remained fixed on Spence's rock-hard jaw and the faint, guileless smile lifting the corners of his mouth.

Fortunately, at that moment the waitress arrived with their drinks, and Claire was spared the necessity of immediately replying to Spence's revelation.

While she sipped her wine, she forced herself to examine what he'd said calmly. Was he teasing her, playing with her? Or was he actually telling her that his being here had something to do with herself? Cautiously, she shot him a surreptitious look over the rim of her wineglass. But at that moment Spence's own eyes flickered sideways and he intercepted her glance. Their gazes locked and held. Claire watched in hypnotized fascination as the green and gold glints in his hazel eyes seemed to dance with humor and warmth. The heat in his look communicated itself to her, running the length of her body and down to her toes so that they curled inside her expensive leather shoes.

During the meal that followed, Spence and his associate kept up a steady patter of light, genial conversation. They asked questions about the area and joked mildly about their difficulties finding their way around the intricate map of Newton with its cul-de-sacs and fanciful street names.

"Yes. I'm told that there's a little old lady with a book of obscure Victorian poets who makes up those street names," Joe told them with a laugh.

"I can believe it," Spence responded, grinning back. "I nearly fell over when I saw that the *Voice*'s office building was located on Celestial Highway."

They all chuckled appreciatively, but behind their polite smiles there was mutual curiosity and speculation. It wasn't, however, until the meal was ended and the foursome had pushed back their plates and ordered coffee that the real purpose of the luncheon was introduced.

Spence gave Claire a direct look. "I've been studying the small-newspaper situation in the area pretty carefully. I have to congratulate you on what you and your staff have accomplished in the last two years. It's impressive."

Claire's eyebrows shot up. "That sounds like you've been reading back issues."

Spence nodded calmly. "Oh, yes. I like to understand a situation before I become involved in it professionally. And I think the best way to size up a community and its newspaper is to trace their development. Chris will tell you that before buying the *Voice*, I read every back copy there was."

"The *Voice* only started up a few years ago, whereas the *Gazette* has been part of this community for decades," Claire said pointedly.

Spence shot her a measuring glance. "That doesn't change the fact that they're both small newspapers serving adjacent communities that have interests in common. Claire, you must know that my corporation has owned and managed a chain of similar publications in the Midwest for years."

She nodded. Claire knew what was coming next, and it was all she could do to keep her hands from clenching on the handle of her fragile coffee cup.

"I intend to get something very similar started in the East," Spence went on. "My staff and I have done a lot of research and we feel this area is ideal for a chain."

Claire put her coffee cup down and very carefully moved the saucer to one side. "And your first move was to buy the *Voice?*"

"Yes, my first move was the purchase of the *Voice,*" Spence confirmed levelly. "It's a young paper, but its staff is enthusiastic and innovative and it's in a prestigious and rapidly growing new city ideally located between two major metropolitan areas. I'm very satisfied with the purchase and now I'm ready to expand. I want to make you an offer for the *Gazette.*"

Claire's gut reaction was to get up and walk out. Selling the *Gazette* would be like selling a piece of herself. She would never agree to it. But there was more bothering her than business. Here, coolly sitting before her, was the man who had seduced her in a matter of hours. In that one impetuous evening she had thrown over the principles of a lifetime. And now, looking the picture of unruffled masculine authority, he was proposing to buy out from under her what she now regarded as her life's work. The effrontery of it kindled a burning sense of outrage deep within her. And she was having a very hard time keeping a lid on it. Claire didn't lose her temper very often. But when she did, it tended to be a fiery display.

Nevertheless, somehow she managed to bottle up her runaway emotions and look at her host with an outwardly calm face. She was a professional, not a temperamental schoolgirl, she told herself. Unlike their last meeting, she would play this confrontation out with her dignity intact.

"What is your proposition?"

Spence leaned forward and put his hands flat on the table. "One I think you'll find is very much to your advantage," he began.

And, as he outlined his offer, Claire had to admit that the terms were more than generous. In exchange for a controlling interest, he held out to Claire the option of staying on as the *Gazette*'s publisher with control over most editorial decisions. His offer would bring her a great deal of money while at the same time allow her to continue in essentially the same fashion she had for the past two years.

Nevertheless, Claire was far from bowled over. Despite her cool, sophisticated façade, she had an emotional, stubborn streak that ran deep. Though he had dressed it up in attractive ribbons, what Spence was maneuvering for was a change of real authority. Claire did not want to be a mere figurehead. That was not what she had given up a fiancé and a very promising career in New York for. Moreover, though he had made no more allusions to their previous relationship, it was still very much in her mind. Somehow she had the feeling that he was proposing to buy not only her paper but herself as well. She would be a puppet whose strings were held by Spence McCabe. Undoubtedly, given what had happened at their first encounter, he imagined she would be at his beck and call in more ways than one. The warm speculative looks he had been bestowing on her all through lunch certainly didn't argue that what he had in mind was a strictly business relationship. And Claire was insulted by the idea. What had happened between them had been a freakish aberration brought on by an unusual situation, she told herself. Maybe she had given the man the impression that she was easily had, but she was not for sale—and if Spence McCabe imagined he could buy her along with her paper, he was in for a rude awakening.

"I guess you don't know my feelings about chains," she began, looking with all the composure she could muster from Spence to his associate and then back again. "I feel strongly that a newspaper should represent the community it serves and that it should be owned and managed locally. Believing that, I couldn't possibly sell the *Gazette* to you." Though she had steeled herself to make her refusal as polite and emotionless as possible, there was unconscious defiance in her voice.

Spence picked it up at once and his brow began to furrow. "I can't believe you've really thought this out carefully," he rumbled. "Have you considered all the advantages that my support could bring?"

"Such as?"

Spence looked at her hard for a long moment, one of his dark brows beginning to move upward in a quizzical arch. "Such as a more stable financial base. These are tough times for newspapers. You must be aware that even large publications with long and notable histories are folding. But there's strength in numbers. A chain can offer advertisers options for a wider and more diversified audience, and it can do the same for classified ads. It can pay for high quality coverage on issues its members have in common. You know how difficult it is to keep topnotch staff on a restricted budget." Spence's green-flecked gaze turned to rest on Joe. All during the negotiations the thin young man had been sitting quietly at Claire's side, taking in the exchange intently. Now he flushed slightly as Spence scrutinized him.

"Your man Vicchio here is an excellent news editor," the publisher continued. "Though he's close to being fresh out of journalism school, he has real ability and it shows in the *Gazette*'s news coverage."

Claire nodded, acknowledging the compliment to Joe and her paper. But she said nothing. What was Spence's angle now?

"How long do you think you're going to be able to keep him?" he challenged. "You know that journalists with talent who take jobs with community publications at the outset of their careers are eventually lured away by bigger papers. A chain has more strength in this area. It can offer its top staff a larger readership, more scope, more prestige, and more money. And in the long run that means higher quality and better service to the reading public."

Claire couldn't keep the scowl off her face that Spence's last argument provoked. Her relationship with her staff, and Joe in particular, was very important to her. She was proud of the judgment she'd shown in recognizing his talents and glad she'd given him the kind of position he deserved. She knew, of course, that someday he would move on. But that was not a prospect she wanted to contemplate at this moment. Spence's argument had struck a sour note, and it was time to put an end to this futile discussion. There was nothing he could say that would make her willing to sell.

While Spence and his cohort eyed her expressionlessly, she thanked them for lunch, wished them luck with the *Voice,* and firmly turned down their offer. "I think we're doing a good job and serving our community well. The *Gazette* has always been independent, and I think it should stay that way," she told them. As quickly as possible after that she excused herself and left the dining room. But all during her measured retreat, she could feel Spence's steady gaze on her back and knew with an irrational mix of fear and elation that he had no intention of accepting her refusal, either personal or professional.

During the luncheon Joe had been uncharacteristically silent. Once they had gained the privacy of her car, however, he opened up.

"Is there something between you and McCabe you're not telling me?"

Claire realized she should have anticipated the question. Joe didn't miss much, and there was no way he could have failed to pick up the unspoken undercurrents between Spence and herself.

Now she gave herself time to answer by making a show of adjusting the rearview mirror before backing out of her parking space. "What are you talking about?" she finally asked with elaborate unconcern.

Joe's answer was not what she had expected. "All through lunch the guy was looking at you like you were an ice cream sundae and he was a hungry kid with a dollar in his pocket."

Claire had to laugh. "Maybe that's the way he looks when he's getting ready to pounce on a potential victim and gobble up another newspaper."

"Yeah, I suppose that was it," Joe agreed before lapsing into a thoughtful silence. And then he shifted on the seat to face Claire. "Are you sure you're making the right decision?" he questioned earnestly.

Claire shot him a startled glance. "What do you mean?"

Joe sighed. "I mean McCabe's offer was generous. And

what he said made a lot of sense. Is it wise to just turn it down out of hand without thinking about it?"

Claire's forehead puckered as she turned left onto the highway that would take them back to Emerson Mills. "I have thought about it, Joe. Though McCabe is very persuasive, I've heard all his arguments before. Have you forgotten that we've just received five awards for excellence? The *Gazette* is doing very well on its own, and I think it will continue to be successful."

Joe averted his dark head to the car's side window and seemed to study the line of trees and sparsely scattered houses set well back from the road that they were now traveling. "I hope you're right," he muttered under his breath. "Because, I have a feeling we haven't seen the last of Spencer C. McCabe."

Claire had that feeling too, and it was confirmed later that evening.

Dressed in jeans and a comfortable mauve sweater with a deep cowl neck, she was trying to get a blaze going in the fireplace when a peremptory tap from the brass door knocker outside warned that she had a visitor.

Hastily dusting some clinging wood chips from her hands, she stood up and smoothed the hipline of her faded denims and then ran a nervous hand through her short hair. It could be almost anyone out there, but some instinct deep within her knew it was Spence. And that intuitive knowledge was proven correct when she hesitantly swung open the heavy wood front door. He was standing squarely in front of her, framed against the darkness by the porch light, one of his hands jammed in the pants pockets of the gray suit he'd worn earlier, a quizzical expression on his strongly cut face. In his free hand he clasped a small package loosely.

She stared up at him silently, unable to think of anything to say.

The quizzical expression deepened. "May I come in?"

Nodding, she swung the door open and stepped aside. He strode across the threshold and then stood looking around the hall and through the archway into the dimly lit living room. "Why do you have candles in your windows?"

"Family tradition," Claire said, briefly explaining the story.

Spence smiled. "You have a lovely home. It isn't what I'd pictured for you, but now that I've seen it, it's just right."

Curiosity was on her face. "What had you pictured?"

The corners of his mouth lifted teasingly. "Something very modern and sleek."

"That just shows you don't know me very well."

Spence shook his head and smiled ruefully. "You didn't give me the chance." Turning, he strode through the archway and into the living room where logs and pieces of kindling and newspaper lay scattered on the small oriental rug in front of the hearth.

"I was just trying to get a fire lit," Claire explained a little nervously as she followed him in. What was he doing here? What was he planning to say?

Spence set the small package down on an end table and gestured at the logs. "Can I help you with that? I've developed a pretty effective technique where fires are concerned."

She couldn't stop herself from reacting to the double meaning. Had it been intentional, she wondered, or was she so on edge where this man was concerned that she was reading mocking little messages into every word he said?

"Please do." She gestured at the cold wood. "I wasn't having any success at all. May I get you a drink or a cup of coffee?" she added as an afterthought.

Spence took off his jacket, hung it over a chair, and then squatted down easily in front of the hearth. The move pulled the material of his pants tight over the solidly muscled hardness of his thighs, and Claire found her gaze wandering appreciatively over their taut outline.

"You could get me a cup of coffee," he said over his shoulder as he began rearranging the logs with the poker. "I'm tired. I've had a long, frustrating day and I need some perking up."

Claire turned on her heel and left the room. Another not very hidden message? she asked herself as she headed into the kitchen. And why was she doing this? She had allowed him to make himself at home in her living room as though they were going to spend the evening here together. Maybe that was what he planned, she thought as she poured water into the coffeemaker and plugged it in. Maybe he even imagined he was going to be spending more than the evening here. Claire eyed the now gurgling appliance mutinously. Well, they were going to have to get some things straight between them, and maybe tonight was the time to do it.

When she reentered the living room there was a crackling fire throwing wavering shadows on the ceiling; and Spence was sprawled on the sofa, his long legs thrust straight out in front of him and his head tipped back so that she could see the strong line of his throat. He hadn't lied about being tired, she admitted. There were dark shadows under his eyes and a fine-edged tension in his face. At the sound of her footsteps he lifted his head and watched silently while she set the tray down on a small table near him.

"Thanks," he murmured, reaching forward and taking one of the steaming cups. "As I said before, it's been a long, frustrating day."

Claire stiffened. "If you're talking about lunch, about my refusing your offer . . ."

Spence raised his hand palm outward to cut short her outburst. "That's not what I want to talk about," he said in his resonant voice. "I came here to discuss something else." He looked at her steadily. "Why did you leave me the way you did? Why did you walk out of my bed and out of my life as though what happened between us meant nothing?"

Claire inhaled sharply and clasped her hands together in an unconsciously prayerful gesture. She had been expecting this, but now that the question was out, it left her with a breathless, hollow feeling.

"Spence," she began awkwardly, her eyes not quite meeting his searching scrutiny, "what happened at that hotel. It wasn't . . . I'm not . . ." She took a deep breath and started again. "It's not the sort of thing I would ever do normally. But I was off-balance that night. I'd had a shock and I was in a state. I wasn't myself," she finished lamely.

Spence reached up, took her hand, and drew her down beside him. "You don't have to tell me that one-night stands aren't your style, Claire. I knew that. I knew that from the beginning."

"You did?" Her eyes searched his. "But how could you? The way I behaved, you had every reason to think . . ."

He put a warm finger on her lips, silencing her. "I had

every reason to think that you were a very beautiful lady and that things had somehow come together to make me a very fortunate man."

His free hand touched her shoulder and then went around to her back, splaying across her flesh so that she could feel his warmth against her backbone and shoulder blades. The sensation was comforting, as though she had been taken into the protection of a strong, benevolent force. And the shadowy, flickering light from the fireplace reinforced the feeling.

"Right now I want to be fortunate again," he murmured huskily, his face very close to hers. And then he was closer yet, his lips brushing hers with seductive tenderness. Back and forth they moved and she was powerless to draw away.

For weeks now she had been remembering his touch, dreaming about it. And now once more it was a spellbinding reality. Everything about this man appealed to her, Claire acknowledged helplessly. The rough texture of his skin next to hers, his clean masculine scent, the power and strength she felt in the shelter of his body—all of it was a drug acting to overwhelm her senses. Despite her earlier intentions, she submitted to his gently controlled embrace without protest. But then the mild demand became more forceful. His lips settled on her mouth firmly, commanding rather than coaxing a response. And Claire could not withhold what he wanted. Perhaps in most ways they were still strangers. But their bodies knew each other's intimately. Being taken into Spence's arms and feeling his mouth on hers was like coming home. His tongue forced its way beyond the yielding line of her lips, and like lovers too long parted their tongues met and entwined in a heated embrace.

After a long moment Spence's head lifted. He looked hungrily down into Claire's half-closed, passion-heated gaze and groaned. "Why did you walk out?" he asked again, more insistently. One large hand slipped beneath the bottom edge of her sweater and began to stroke the smooth flesh of her midriff. She trembled beneath the rhythmic suggestion of the simple caress. But while her body was still reacting to the hypnotic effect of Spence's overpowering closeness, her mind was struggling valiantly to free itself from the spell his body had cast over hers. Deliberately, his hand moved up to close over the soft mound of her breast, his slightly rough thumb erotically circling the nipple. And Claire gasped at the effort it cost her not to reach out and pull him closer.

"Why?" he repeated yet again.

Why had she walked out on him? For many very good reasons, Claire reminded herself. Thinking back on her impetuous behavior, a flush began to color her face. It was prompted now by embarrassment rather than passion. What was this scene on the couch but a replay of her former behavior? This man had walked in the door only a few minutes earlier, and here she was in front of a fire giving herself to him again. Only now it was in her home instead of a hotel, and she hadn't been drinking anything stronger than tea. She had no excuse this time. What's more, she had every reason to suspect his motives. He was trying to take her paper away, for God's sake!

Claire went rigid in his arms and began to push at his invading hands. "Let go of me, Spence! This is crazy!"

But his grip only tightened, and he searched the expression on her flushed face with a deepening frown. "Stop playing games with me, Claire. I like this kind of craziness and so do you," he rasped.

There was nothing she could say to that. How could she deny that she'd been enjoying herself just now? Caught in the mindless excitement he seemed to generate in her so effortlessly, she'd been lost to all the good sense that normally ruled her actions. But no more! Her head was back in charge now and things were going to stay that way!

She made a determined effort to sit up and this time he let her slip from his grasp. Springing away from the couch, she walked agitatedly to the fire and stood looking down at it with her back to him.

"We're both adults," she muttered loud enough for him to hear. "We both know that I was bent out of shape that night. You might as well know—I'd just been ditched by my fiancé, and I'd had too much to drink. Your timing happened to be perfect, and that's why we wound up in bed together. As they say in the song," she added with a humorless twist, "it was just one of those things." She almost choked on the humiliating words, but somehow she managed to get them out. Unconsciously, she laced her fingers together. Despite the heat thrown by the fire, they were trembling with cold.

And then her body jerked with alarm as she felt Spence's hands clasp her shoulders and spin her body around to face him as though she were a weightless doll. "Are you saying our lovemaking meant nothing to you?" His features as he spoke were set, and his eyes, which moments before had looked down at her with such passionate desire, were like green-flecked ice.

Claire's gaze dropped. "No, I'm not saying that," she mumbled. "It did mean something to me. I'm not in the habit of falling into bed with strangers. But I have to think it wasn't that special for you." And then she set her teeth and looked up at him defiantly. "While you were sleeping beside me, you even called out another woman's name!"

A jolt of electricity seemed to shoot down Claire's spine like a warning signal as she watched the change of expression on Spence's face. He had been looking at her with barely controlled anger and his hands had been locked tightly on her shoulders. But at her words his face went completely still. Some of the color seeped from it, and his large hands loosened and fell away from her rigid body. A heavy silence hung suspended in the air between them, and suddenly Claire was painfully aware of the superheated wood in the fireplace crackling and bursting like enemy gunshots.

"I called out a name?"

She nodded stiffly, determined not to back down now that she'd brought the subject up.

"Whose name?" he asked very quietly. "Whose name did I call?"

"You called for Kathleen," she told him.

He turned then and stood in a posture that seemed all wrong for him. His massive shoulders sagged slightly and his arms hung limply at his sides. "I'm sorry," he said in a toneless voice. And then he picked up his jacket, slung it over his arm, and walked out of the room.

When Claire heard the front door close behind him, she could only stare helplessly into the empty space he'd occupied a moment before. She felt as though something very important had happened, and she'd only half understood it.

When she heard the motor of his car spring to life outside, she ran to the window and peered out into the night. But all she could see were the taillights of a car pulling out onto the main road and then disappearing.

With an inexplicable feeling of despair, she turned and stared blindly around the silent, empty room. And then her gaze focused on the package he'd left on the table. Moving closer, she looked down and saw her name written on the paper wrapping. When she'd undone it, she didn't know whether to laugh or cry. It was the underwear she'd been unable to find in Spence's hotel room, laundered and neatly folded.

CHAPTER FIVE

Two months later Claire was studying a press release when Sheila Smythe's crisp voice floated over the intercom. "Mr. McCabe on line two."

While her forehead creased, Claire's finger hovered for a moment over the telephone's blinking plastic square. What can he want? she wondered. Of course, he might be calling to discuss some matter of business. But chances were the conversation would end the way it always seemed to. After that first puzzling evening with Spence in her living room, he had not approached her for nearly three weeks. But then he had started to call, inviting her to spend time with him for every conceivable reason. She had continually turned him down.

Yet, despite her dogged refusals, she was not able to avoid seeing a lot of him. He seemed to have a sixth sense as to her whereabouts. She inevitably ran into him at every press conference, every public function, and every party she attended. And always he managed to have a few private words with her.

At the opening of the new firehouse, for example, he neatly maneuvered her into a lengthy discussion of the cable TV system that was about to invade the county.

"Well, I just hope they keep the late-night porn off the

77

pay channels," she'd protested without realizing where her words might lead. "It may be okay for you people in Newton. But it's definitely not appropriate for most of the county."

Spence's rich laugh had brought her back to reality. "Do I take it that you see Newton as the Sodom and Gomorrah of Blake County?" he'd challenged. "Well, I certainly hope that's not the way you see me, because if it is, I want to assure you that I'm really a pretty clean-living guy." He paused significantly and then added, "Except when the temptation is too overwhelming to resist."

Claire had flushed and looked away from the message in his hazel eyes. She realized exactly what he was doing now. If he couldn't inveigle her in a private conversation, he was going to fill his public remarks with private meaning. But she wasn't going to let him get to her that way.

Skillfully she buttonholed and drew the fire commissioner into the conversation and then excused herself to greet an old friend from *The Baltimore Sun*.

Yet, being continually on her guard against Spence McCabe took a lot of effort, because she wasn't fighting only him. She was also fighting her own treacherous inclinations. Whenever he spoke to her—whether the topic was politics, the arts, or even the weather—she couldn't help being caught up in his every word. And the interest wasn't just superficial. Something in the man called to a part of her that had long been unsatisfied. But despite her unwilling fascination with him, she still managed to keep her distance because she felt that was essential to keeping her self-respect.

Knowing that he was waiting to speak to her now made her palms grow cold. Maybe she should simply inform

Sheila that she was always "out of the office" to Mr. McCabe.

But, no, she couldn't do that. As the publisher of *The Newton Voice,* he might well have legitimate business. And besides, all her feminine instincts told her that to openly snub him would be a dangerous course. He might escalate the covert skirmishes that had been going on between them for weeks into all-out war. She didn't want that—for herself or for the *Emerson Mills Gazette.*

Sighing, she pressed the button and picked up the receiver. "Yes?" she said, her voice unconsciously wary.

"I'd hoped for a warmer welcome," Spence's gravelly tones came over the line. Despite herself, at the sound of his voice she felt a warm prickle of sensation at the back of her neck. Why did the man have to affect her this way? She damned herself. At their frequent meetings during the past month and a half, she had had to exercise tremendous control to keep her outward demeanor cool. Despite all her refusals, he still wanted her. He made that clear in everything he did—the way he looked at her across crowded rooms, the double meanings simmering beneath the surface of his polite conversation, the caress of his deep voice on all her nerve endings when he called with one of his frequent invitations. She'd always managed to refuse before. But this time Spence's ploy was too clever for Claire to evade.

"I've been talking to Bert Patterson," he began. At the mention of the county manager, Claire pricked up her ears. "He has a new pet project—barrier-free entrances for all public buildings to accommodate the handicapped," Spence began. "He wants some publicity. Of course, it flashed through my mind that a private meeting would be a good opportunity for the new publisher on the block to curry some favor." Spence chuckled. "But then my more gentlemanly side prevailed. I knew you'd be interested too, so I told him I'd set up a meeting with the three of us. When would be a good time for you?"

For a moment Claire was speechless. Intimate little meetings with Spencer McCabe were things she'd been doing her best to avoid. The chemical reaction between them was so powerful that every time she laid eyes on the man her composure was wrecked. On the other hand, how would it look if she refused? Bert Patterson was touchy and might well take offense if she sent one of her underlings to hear about a project he was personally sponsoring. And his displeasure could mean he'd "forget" to send important press releases to the *Gazette*. She had been neatly cornered.

"How thoughtful of you," she clipped into the phone. They both knew that in their private war Spence had just outflanked her.

Under the circumstances he could afford to let her seem to set the terms. There was a note of warm satisfaction in his voice. "Naturally, since I couldn't consult you, I told him the meeting would have to be set up at your convenience. What time is good for you?"

Claire glanced down at the large calendar on her neatly arranged desk. It gave her a perverse satisfaction to note that almost every day this week was filled with appointments. "I'm afraid I'm all booked up for the next several days," she returned sweetly. "If you want a meeting with all three of us, I'm afraid you'll have to wait until next Monday.

"Monday it is then," Spence came back briskly. "What time?"

Claire took a shot in the dark. "Eleven o'clock?"

"Fine by me," Spence agreed. "I'll call you back if there's any problem with Patterson."

There was no problem with the appointment. But Claire soon realized she had made a mistake in setting the date so far in advance. It gave her time to brood about Spence and to work up a case of nerves about being in his company. It wasn't so bad during the day when she could keep busy. But at night when she was free from thoughts of business, inevitably Spence would once more fill her mind. She tried to tell herself that she was simply worried about how his takeover of the *Voice* might affect the *Gazette*. But she was too honest to fool herself that way for long.

It was true that in the first weeks since he'd come to Newton she had been apprehensive about the impact on her paper. Would Spence launch an all-out campaign to wipe out the *Gazette*? Would he try to undercut her ad prices to wipe out her revenues or try to scoop her on all the best stories to make her look second-rate? So far, none of these things had happened. Spence was apparently not as impetuous in business as he was in love. He was taking a wait-and-see approach and using his time to get to know the county and the community where she had no doubt he eventually planned to make his mark.

But in her heart she knew this was not her real concern. It was the mark he'd left on her that really had her running scared. Alone in the dark she could vividly remember the feel of his hands and lips on her body and the tumultuous response he had elicited from her. If her memories were devastating, the reality of Spencer McCabe's large masculine frame lounging indolently in the intimacy of Bert Patterson's small, paneled office wreaked complete havoc on Claire.

The day the appointment was scheduled, she'd once

again been careful to dress in a businesslike blazer and skirt ensemble. The weather was cool enough now for her to wear high leather boots. But they were hardly armor against the X ray quality of Spence's searching glance when she entered the room. As his hazel eyes looked her up and down, it was as though he was remembering her naked body in his bed. And she could not help responding to the warmth of that covetous look.

Beneath her sober exterior every nerve ending was vibrantly aware of him. It took all her willpower to shake Bert Patterson's hand. While she stood there exchanging pleasantries with the balding, stoop-shouldered county manager, she could feel Spence's gaze like a physical touch on the back of her neck.

Bert was unaware of the tension between the two publishers he had invited to hear about his new proposal. Jovially, he offered them coffee and then pulled out a series of architectural drawings showing how county buildings and parking lots could easily be altered to accommodate people in wheelchairs. "We can't deny so many of our citizens access to their public officials," Bert declared, waving his scarecrow-thin arms with fervor.

"Yes," Spence agreed wholeheartedly. "It's a terrible thing to be denied access."

His gaze sought Claire's. But she looked down into her coffee cup while she tried not to choke on the hot liquid she had been in the process of swallowing.

"I hope you'll print these pictures," Bert plowed on with energetic cheer. "They'll illustrate just how frustrating it must be not to get where you want to go."

"Indeed," Spence agreed, leaning forward to examine the renderings more carefully. "You've got a sympathizer in me. I know all about frustration."

That was too much. Claire shot him a murderous glare which he met with a bland smile, his brown-green eyes catching a shaft of sun from the window and beginning to glint.

"What are your thoughts on frustration, Claire?" he asked smoothly.

She could feel a flush composed of equal parts of anger and embarrassment creeping up her neck. Claire fought to hold on to her equanimity. She would not give Spencer McCabe the satisfaction of knowing just how expertly his jibes were hitting the mark. And she certainly wasn't going to let Bert Patterson in on the double entendres.

Turning determinedly away from her gentle tormentor, she addressed her remarks to the county manager. "The *Gazette* will be happy to do a story on this," she informed him. "I'm glad you called it to our attention."

As the minutes crept by, the threesome went on to discuss the issue more fully. Claire pulled out a leather-bound pad and jotted down a few quick notes. By the time the meeting was concluded, she had gotten the name of the architectural firm involved and promised to send a reporter over to do an interview.

When she rose to leave, however, Spence was right behind her. Accompanying her out the door, he put his hand on her arm as they reached the corridor.

"What's the hurry?" he questioned. "How about another cup of coffee in the cafeteria downstairs?"

Through the material of her jacket she was very much aware of his large fingers gripping her flesh. Her instinct was to jerk away, but she had too much pride to let him see so clearly how he affected her. Instead, she went on the defensive. "I don't want another cup of coffee. I've got enough acid churning around in my stomach as it is. Just what were you trying to accomplish in Patterson's office anyway?"

The big man, striding easily along at her side, stopped in his tracks and turned her toward him. "I think you know very well what I was trying to do." His eyes sought and held her gaze. "When are you going to stop this game you've been playing with me? I want to see you, Claire; and I think you want to see me too. Why the big runaround?"

Claire's nervous gaze shot skittishly around the busy corridor. Too many of the people here knew who she was. And this was hardly the place to discuss their personal relationship.

Spence took in the meaning of her reaction immediately and sighed. "My car is just outside. Sit in it with me for a minute so we can talk in privacy."

He was already leading her out the door before she could protest. And there was no way she could extricate herself from his determined grasp without making even more of a scene.

To her surprise, when they were out of the building, he led her to a battered blue station wagon stuffed with lumber in various lengths. It was parked in the relatively private lot in back of the red brick county office building. When he saw her eyeing the car doubtfully, Spence grinned. "I'm making some improvements on my new town house, and I thought I might as well stop by the lumberyard on my way here. But don't worry, the front is pretty clear."

To demonstrate, he opened the door and shooed her onto the bench seat. Claire sat for a moment, looking askance at the press releases, old newspapers, and woodworking tools that cluttered the floor at her feet.

"Sorry, as you can see, I'm not the neat-as-a-pin type," Spence explained equably as he slid in next to her behind the steering wheel.

"I can see that," Claire agreed.

"Maybe what I need is a woman to organize my life. And I wish you'd take a shot at the job, Claire."

She stared at him in open-mouthed surprise. That sounded almost like an old-fashioned proposal. She must not have understood him right.

"Why have you been giving me the cold shoulder like this?" he went on, ignoring her confusion. "You know how much I want to see you. Surely I've made that perfectly plain."

"Oh, yes," Claire conceded. "You've made yourself clear on that. You want to take up where we left off. But I have no intention of letting that happen."

Spence turned toward her and slid his arm along the top of the seat in back of her. His face, as he studied her closed expression, was a mixture of frustration and determination.

"Why not?" His voice went down a tone. "Did you think I was the type to make love and run?" Spence's mouth twisted wryly. "Well, obviously, all the running I did was in your direction." His hand went to the back of her neck, stroking the thick feather-cut hair he found there. It had suddenly become impossible for Claire to concentrate on his words. Her attention was concentrated on the warm sensations he was producing on the sensitive flesh at the base of her skull. While his fingers combed through the short tendrils of hair, she momentarily gave herself up to the pleasure of his touch.

He had no trouble recognizing the small surrender. "I know we started out too quickly," he murmured in a warm dark voice, his clean breath fanning her cheek as his fingers caught her chin and turned her face up to his. "We'll make up for it," he went on, "by starting again. And this time we'll take it slow."

If Spence hadn't been so overpoweringly close, Claire might have been able to pull back and challenge his male logic. But the look in his eyes and the feel of his hands had sabotaged her will. As his face lowered to hers, her eyes closed and she submitted mindlessly to the intoxication of his kiss. Involuntarily, her lips parted and she sighed as she felt his mouth explore the line of hers. Spence's hand slipped to the back of her head again, holding her close. And his other arm went around her shoulder so that she was folded to him in a tight embrace.

Once more the very rocklike strength and size of the man both overwhelmed and reassured her. The woman in her knew that in his arms she could come to no harm from the outside world. The image might seem outmoded in the twentieth century, but she couldn't help thinking of him as a fortress of male invincibility guarding her vulnerable femininity. How could she deny him anything he wanted? And what she wanted, as well?

As his tongue explored the honeyed sweetness of her mouth, her hands crept to his shoulders, taking in the rough tweedy texture of his jacket and the solid feel of the heavily muscled shoulders beneath.

Spence's lips had begun their own exploration. They moved across the line of her jaw and then paused to nip gently at the gold stud in her earlobe. "Claire, just holding you in my arms like this feels so good. I can't tell you how much I've missed you. Why have you have been denying us this pleasure?"

Claire had no answer for that question. She could only

respond to the overwhelming feelings that Spence was kindling so easily.

Rhythmically, Spence stroked her shoulder and then her back. When she felt his hand move to the front of her body and slide underneath her jacket, she unconsciously moved back so that he could cup her breasts. A thrill shot through her at his touch. Helplessly she felt the soft globes beneath her silk blouse tauten with the excitement he was generating. And she knew he was equally aware of her strong response.

But when she felt his fingers begin to ease open the pearl buttons, she knew things were going too far. "Spence, you must stop," she whispered urgently, suddenly once more aware that they were in a public parking lot.

Ignoring her protest, his hand slid inside the thin silk and his fingers found the warm curve of flesh at the top of her bra. Claire inhaled sharply, her breath hissing between her teeth. She was a seething cauldron of conflicting emotions now. Her flesh was aching with desire. She wanted him to go on, but she knew he must stop. "Spence, you have to quit," she pleaded, pushing ineffectually at his shoulders. Her power to resist was fast melting under his sensual onslaught. Spence knew it too. Lifting his face, he looked deeply into her flushed face. "You want me as much as I want you," he accused huskily. And it was true. If they had been alone in her house instead of in a parked car, she would have yielded. But this was not the place for such intimacies.

As if to confirm that fact, the intrusive sound of male laughter suddenly assaulted Claire's ears. Both she and Spence stiffened and looked up to see a group of four briefcase-toting lawyers round the corner of the building.

They seemed to be heading toward the Mercedes parked next to Spence's station wagon.

Like a boy caught with his fingers in the cookie jar, Spence jerked back, freeing his hand from Claire's blouse. She felt herself turn bright red as she hastily pulled the front of her jacket closed and buttoned it over her open silk shirt.

The casually joking foursome had reached the Mercedes and, to her horror, Claire recognized two of the men. They greeted her, shooting curious, assessive looks into Spence's disreputable car. And it was all she could do to keep from looking as guilty and embarrassed as she felt. Would their laughter be directed at her and Spence next? she wondered. Suddenly, against her will, the front page of the *Gazette* flashed into her mind. Emblazoned across the top was the headline "EDITOR ARRESTED FOR INDECENT EXPOSURE IN COURTHOUSE PARKING LOT." Claire would have laughed at the absurdity of it if she hadn't been in such turmoil. Instead, she winced.

The minute the Mercedes backed out and pulled away she reached for the door handle of Spence's car. But he grabbed her elbow to keep her in place.

"My God, Claire, I'm sorry. That was my fault. I would never—"

She cut him off with a derisive laugh. "But you did," she flung in his face. Channeling her embarrassment into anger was the easiest course now. "You've just had a very graphic demonstration of why I've been avoiding you," she continued, her voice rising despite her effort to control it. "I have a certain reputation in this town. And I have every intention of protecting it." She was aware she must sound ridiculously prim and prissy. But she couldn't help that now. "If word of this little incident gets around, just how do you think my readers will react?"

"They may just think you're human," Spence clipped out, his own anger fueled by hers. "And while we're on the subject, what exactly do you want them to think about you—that you're some sort of saint? Most unmarried women your age are interested in the opposite sex and do date men, you know."

"Is necking in your car your idea of a date?" Claire shot back furiously. "Really, I thought most men outgrew that after high school!"

Spence's neck went a dull red and he clenched his jaw. When her hand went back to the handle of the door he made no move to stop her. She climbed out, slamming the door behind her. But as she stalked across the parking lot toward her own car, she was painfully aware that her blouse was still unbuttoned beneath her jacket. There was no way to remedy that now. The only thing she could do was clutch her briefcase across her chest like a shield.

Claire was too upset by the incident to go back to the office. Instead, she drove home where she called Joe Vicchio and briefly filled him in on the press conference. Pleading a headache, she told him she'd be out that afternoon. As she replaced the receiver in its cradle, she realized her hand was shaking. It had taken all her strength to keep that tremor out of her voice when she'd talked to Joe. But now she gave in and thought about what had happened. After filling the tea kettle and putting it on the stove she kicked off her shoes and sat down heavily at the kitchen table.

She had put all the blame for the embarrassing incident on Spence. But if she was honest with herself, she would admit she had been as much at fault as he. There was no way around it. She had responded to his touch like dry kindling to a lightning bolt. What was it about the man that induced her to make a fool of herself every time he came within striking range?

Agitated, she began drumming her fingers on the table while she tried to make sense of her tangled feelings. She didn't like the way she had fallen into his bed the first time they'd met. It hurt her pride and cheapened her self-image. She'd told Spence she had to protect her reputation in Emerson Mills. But that was only part of it. How could she have a sexual relationship with the publisher of a rival paper without compromising her integrity? And then there was the way Spence had reacted to the name Kathleen when she'd complained about his murmuring it in his sleep. Obviously there were other women in his life. Claire simply wasn't willing to deal with that sort of relationship. She wasn't going to be one of a collection in any man's life! No, there were just too many questions about this man and his motives.

But one of those questions was answered for Claire the following evening—after the *Gazette* had gone to press. She was just gathering up a bunch of photographs to send back to the files, when Joe emerged from layout, rolling down his shirt sleeves.

"If you're going to use your news editor as an emergency paste-up artist, maybe you'd better give him a bonus," he quipped.

Claire grinned back. She'd had to force him into service because Jeanie, one of her key layout people, had been called home to take care of a sick child just when they were pulling together the news story flats.

"You were noble this afternoon and you do deserve a

reward," she observed. "How about letting me buy you a drink at Ethan's?"

Looking considerably mollified, Joe tugged at the side of his mustache. "As a matter of fact, that's where I was heading," he admitted, slipping into his plaid sports jacket. "You said you wanted to meet some of the new people at the *Voice,* and this will be a good chance for you."

Claire stiffened. Would Spence be there? she wondered. But Joe answered her question before she asked. "I'm getting together with Joyce Rushing and Paul Burton. He's a former investigative reporter Spence hired away from Bill Emory in D.C."

Claire almost sighed with relief. "That sounds great. Just let me get rid of these photos." Scooping up the pile on her desk, she turned toward the file boxes. But as she sorted through the folders there, she thought about what Joe had just told her. Bill Emory's organization had a national reputation. If Spence was hiring his people, he must be sinking a lot of money into the *Voice.* The information nagged at her. Why was he making this kind of investment? What did he have in mind? The question was still running through her head when Joe pushed open the brass-studded swinging door at Ethan's.

It was a lively after-hours gathering place for local professional people. Dim lighting, natural wood surfaces, stained glass, and leafy green hanging plants gave it an attractively relaxed ambience. When Claire and Joe walked in, the place was already humming with the buzz of voices and the clink of cocktail and beer glasses.

"Joyce and Paul said they'd try and get a table in the corner," Joe muttered as he stood on tiptoe and craned his neck to catch sight of his friends. In the next moment he waved at a petite blonde and a tall thin young man and then propelled Claire in their direction.

After introductions had been made all around and another pitcher of beer ordered, Claire studied Joyce Rushing surreptitiously. She had admired the young woman's work, but this was the first time she'd met the attractive blonde. Did Spence find her attractive too? she found herself wondering. And then her eyebrows snapped together. What was she doing asking herself such questions?

Joe shot her a searching stare. "What are you thinking about, Claire? You look like you're about to write an angry editorial."

Claire flushed, but managed a quick recovery. "Oh, I was just reminded of something stupid that happened yesterday."

"Was it that press conference with Bert Patterson?" Joyce inquired. "I don't know what happened, but Spence was certainly in a bad mood when he came back. And that's unusual. Normally he's a doll around the office, but he was barking orders like a drill sergeant all yesterday afternoon." Joyce chuckled indulgently, a warm glow lighting her eyes.

But Claire was too busy fighting the blush spreading across her cheeks to notice the way Joyce smiled when she talked about Spence. Claire was thankful that the lighting in Ethan's was dim. "No, it wasn't the press conference," she said. "What did you do before coming to this area?" she asked the young woman in an attempt to change the subject.

Joyce finished her mug of ale and refilled her glass from the pitcher in the center of the table. "I worked for *Harbor Lights* magazine in Baltimore. Actually, I was thinking about going back there before Spence took over. But I couldn't give up having a boss like him. You wouldn't believe the editorial instincts that man has. He knows just when to give his people free rein."

"And when you need direction," Paul Burton chimed in. He laughed. "I like working for the guy too," he added, "but I'm not the all-out fan Joyce is." He shot the blonde a sly, teasing look. "I think she's fallen in love with him."

Joyce jabbed her elbow into Paul's skinny ribs. "Oh, come on! Can't a woman admire a man without being in love with him? Besides, I'd have to be crazy to go for Spence McCabe. He's still carrying a giant-sized torch for his wife."

Claire's knuckles whitened around her beer mug. "His wife . . ." she repeated.

"Her name was Kathleen," Joyce supplied helpfully. "She died a couple years back—of a heart condition. She was sick for a long time. That's why he doesn't have any kids. But he must have been crazy about her because as far as I know he hasn't so much as looked at another woman since her death."

CHAPTER SIX

The rest of the evening at Ethan's went by in a haze for Claire. She could only listen to the table chatter around her with half an ear. Though she managed to nod and smile as though she were really participating, her mind was somewhere else. Finally, pleading fatigue, she excused herself early and headed back home. As she pulled out of her parking space and maneuvered her white coupe out into the Friday evening traffic, her mind was on what she'd learned about Spence.

After her recent encounter with the man, she thought she had settled their relationship—or non-relationship—in her mind. But Joyce's revelations had added a whole new dimension. Apparently, Spence was not the type who chased anything in skirts. He had singled her out and pursued her with a relentless tenacity that was rare for him.

At last she understood his murmured words. "It's been so long." If a man of his virility had been without a woman since his wife died two years ago, then it really had been a long time. She supposed she should be flattered that he wanted her in particular. And she was. But still she wondered what Spence really felt toward her. After they'd made love, the name on his lips was not Claire but Kathleen, she recalled with a wince of pain.

Claire was jerked from her reverie by the realization that she'd missed her own driveway. It just showed how much this situation was affecting her, she admitted with a rueful shake of her dark head. Pulling to the side of the road, she waited until it was safe to make a U turn and then nosed her car back toward home.

The truth was, all her feminine instincts and desires clamored to let Spence renew the relationship. She did want to see him again. And more than just see him, she admitted honestly, she wanted to feel his arms around her, his lips on hers. But, at the same time, the rational part of her brain was issuing warnings. It wasn't just her reputation and her self-respect that Spence threatened, but her emotions. In New York she had been making love on the rebound. But though she hadn't known it at the time, so was he. Surprisingly, he had wiped all thoughts of Richard from her mind. But she had obviously not done the same for him. Had there really been three people in that passion-tossed bed—she, Spence, and Kathleen's ghost?

Sighing heavily, Claire opened the front door and flipped on the hall light. All at once she felt so weary that she wondered if she would be able to climb the steps to bed. Instead she sank down into one of the high-backed Queen Anne chairs on either side of her fireplace and kicked off her shoes.

The chairs were covered in blue velvet. And Claire remembered vividly her father's reaction when he'd come home to find Rose had changed the original worn crewel fabric that Claire's mother had selected for them. "I don't want anything of Ellen's changed," he had bellowed. And

Rose had burst into tears and fled up the stairs to her room.

My mother died young, but she never left this house or Dad's heart, Claire reflected. *And Rose had to live with the knowledge that she was second best as far as Dad was concerned all their married life.* Claire ran her finger thoughtfully along the soft fabric covering the arm of the chair. When her stepmother had moved out, Claire had offered her the chairs, but the older woman had refused them. "Nothing in this house was ever really mine," she'd demurred ruefully. And now Claire, in a way she never had before, could understand what Rose's feelings must have been. She had settled for second place in her husband's heart. *But I don't think I could,* Claire told herself. Would a relationship with Spence be like that? She didn't know the answer. If she was part of his reason for coming to Newton, then he was certainly chasing her as though she meant something more than a one-night stand to him. But she didn't know what to think anymore. She just didn't know.

Over the next few days, despite all her doubts, Claire watched the telephone, wishing that Spence would call. And when the *Voice* came out on Wednesday, she studied it with new interest—looking for Spence's influence. He'd written an editorial supporting a citizens' group that was trying to locate a hospice in the new city. As she read his well-chosen words, she was impressed by the incisive power of his arguments. Most hospitals, he explained, were oriented toward saving patients. When doctors and nurses had to give up on the terminally ill, they often cut off emotional support to the dying patient as well. Was he speaking from his experience with Kathleen? she asked herself. Moved by his vivid description, she found herself wanting desperately to reach out and comfort him. It was all she could do not to pick up the phone and call.

Finally turning the page, she forced herself to assess the *Voice*'s new appearance. The type faces and the graphics were bolder. And the photographs were of higher quality than she remembered. She'd heard that Spence had installed a costly new photo lab, and obviously the expense was paying off. The stories, too, had a new sparkle. Paul Burton could really write, she saw, scanning an article he'd done on a brutality charge at the county jail. And Spence was clearly making good use of the young man's investigative background.

Claire frowned when she began assessing the number and dimensions of the ads the *Voice* was pulling in. Spence had obviously increased the size of his business staff too. She was going to have to stay on her toes to compete with him. And whatever her personal feelings about the man, he was still a formidable business rival. She had better keep that fact firmly in mind.

The next afternoon Claire called a meeting of her staff to discuss the competition.

"I assume you've all been reading the *Voice* lately," she began.

There was a chorus of groans from around the room.

"Yes, as a matter of fact," Joe answered for the group. "I've made our competition 'must' reading for everyone on the staff who wants to keep his job."

"Well, you should have included me," Claire complained lightly. "I can see we really have to give some serious thought to livening up our format and beefing up the ad sales if we're going to keep the wolf, or I mean the *Voice*, at bay."

Though there were some chuckles at her attempt at

humor, the tone of the meeting was serious. The rest of the afternoon was spent brainstorming various strategies. Pamela Lyons, from the sports staff, came up with the idea of running a contest with free subscriptions as prizes. Craig Williams, from advertising, suggested giving merchants a discount for volume. And feature writer Paul Lansing offered a program for involving local highschoolers in a teen page. Though Claire greeted these suggestions enthusiastically, she privately wondered if any of them was innovative enough to meet the threat Spence was now beginning to pose to the *Gazette*'s supremacy in the county. Had she made a mistake in turning down his generous offer of a merger? Claire asked herself. But the answer in her mind was still a clear no. Without autonomy the *Gazette* was nothing, she argued fiercely. And yet, maybe there was some way that the two of them could cooperate. It was worth a try.

And that was why, she told herself, she dug up back issues of the *Voice* so she could read all of Spence's editorials. They were as fascinating as the man and gave her an insight into his character that she'd never really had before. Hospices weren't the only topic he felt strongly about. He had decided opinions on everything from nuclear war to the local swim teams. And on many of those issues she found herself agreeing with his forcefully expressed words. She had been deeply attracted to him before. But now that she knew some of his innermost thoughts, he was even more appealing. On several occasions she had to stop herself from picking up the phone to argue a point with him.

Ironically, when she did pick up the phone and call him, it was about an issue that affected the *Gazette*, not her personally.

Claire had been planning a major feature on Judge Turnbull, a revered member of the local aristocracy famed for having donated his private collection of literary classics to the county library system. He had retired from the circuit court several years ago and had been working on a history of the county ever since. It would be coming out within the month. And locally that was big news. But when one of Claire's feature writers had contacted him about doing a major piece on the book, he'd regretfully explained that he'd already promised an exclusive interview to the *Voice*.

"Are you sure you told them you'd give them an exclusive?" Claire had fished, hoping the white-haired old patriarch had misunderstood his commitment to the rival paper.

"For old time's sake, I'd rather it be you than that other paper," he declared. "But I got so excited about doing an interview on my pet project that I didn't stop to think."

Claire had tried not to sound discouraged. "I'll get back to you later," she told him. "I think I can work something out with the publisher over there."

Even though she had been looking for an excuse to contact Spence, calling took all of Claire's nerve. As she waited for his secretary to announce her name, she could feel her heart thumping in her chest like a drum.

When she finally heard his deep, resonant "And to what do I owe the pleasure of this phone call?" it was all she could do to stay in control of her voice.

"Actually, you owe it to Judge Turnbull," she began, forcing herself to start out on a light note.

"I suspected you might not like my getting the jump on you," Spence acknowledged. "But business is business."

"Yes, well . . ." Claire made herself continue. "I was wondering if we could work something out."

"Go on," the *Voice*'s publisher invited smoothly.

Claire realized that she had made her call before really thinking out a proposal. "In fairness, you should let us do that interview," she blurted. "After all, it's the kind of thing the *Gazette* should run. Judge Turnbull is practically a county institution. And he even tried to block the sale of land to develop Newton. Why would the *Voice* be interested in featuring him?"

"Because we're trying to woo county readers, of course," Spence pointed out with unerring logic. "And besides, if he's willing to let us do the interview, his attitude must have changed somewhat, wouldn't you say?" He paused for a moment and Claire could hear the silence crackling over the phone lines between them.

Was that his last word on the subject? she wondered. She guessed it had been stupid of her to make a personal appeal to him. That he was greeting her overture so coolly said a lot about the status of their relationship. The realization gave Claire an odd, hollow feeling in her chest. Obviously, she had made a mistake, and the best thing to do would be to ring off quickly.

She was about to do just that, when he cleared his throat. "Tell you what—maybe you do have a point. But if you want to argue your case, have lunch with me. I'll pick you up at noon."

Before she could respond, he hung up.

True to his word, he showed up at Claire's office promptly at twelve. But to her surprise he was carrying a paper bag loaded with sandwiches and a thermos of coffee.

"I was planning on something more conventional," he

explained. "But when I stepped outside and saw what glorious weather we're having, I decided it might be fun to eat outdoors. You know Emerson Mills better than I. Can you suggest a good spot?"

Claire was taken with the idea immediately. It really was a beautiful day. Even though the calendar read late November, the temperatures were in the high sixties and the sky was a cloudless, perfect blue. "There's a trail along the river that runs beside our building," she offered. "And there are benches now and then."

"That sounds ideal," Spence agreed as he shepherded her through the office door. And it *was* ideal as they strolled along the cinder path enjoying the unseasonable temperatures and the bubbling rush of the green water as it flowed over the boulder-strewn riverbed.

"Up in Michigan when I think of water I think of lakes. But rivers are where you Marylanders find your water recreation, aren't they?" Spence ventured conversationally.

Claire grinned. "You're right about that. When we were kids we used to innertube right along here. And by the time I was a teenager, we graduated to canoes. That's one reason why I like seeing it outside my office window. It reminds me of what a great childhood I had."

Spence paused near a trailside bench and looked down at her thoughtfully. "Did you have a happy childhood, Claire?"

She nodded. "Yes, I did. Maybe that's why I want to keep Emerson Mills the way it is. I want the kids coming along to have the same advantages I did. You know you can still go down to Main Street now and sit in the soda parlor. And our town is one of the few places in the area where it's still safe to walk at night."

Spence nodded as they both sat down on the bench. "In a way I envy you," he admitted, fishing in the bag for a napkin to use as a tablecloth. Pulling out several sandwiches wrapped in waxed paper, he set them on the napkin between them. "You have your choice of chicken salad or ham and cheese," he informed his guest.

"I'll take the ham," she said, suddenly ravenously hungry from the fresh air. While he poured steaming coffee into a plastic foam cup, she unwrapped a sandwich and took a healthy bite. "What kind of a childhood did you have?" she asked as she accepted the cup from his hand.

Spence began to unwrap his own sandwich, and his hazel eyes took on a reminiscent glow. "I had a good childhood too, though it was different from yours. My father was an autoworker, and my family lived in Detroit. A trip to the country was always a special occasion for me and my brother."

Claire was curious. "Is the J in SJM for your middle name, or is that your brother?"

"It's for my brother, Jimmy," he informed her. And then he began to chuckle. "My middle initial is C—for Commodus. My mother wanted us to have middle names of Roman emperors, and since I was such a big baby, she picked that name for me."

Claire couldn't help laughing out loud. "How many people know what the C stands for?"

Spence rolled his sandwich wrapper up and stuffed it back into the bag. "Not many," he admitted. "It's not something I tell everyone. I think Jimmy got the better of the deal. He's James Tiberius."

"So the two of you are partners," she prompted, putting away her own sandwich wrapper and taking another sip of coffee.

Spence leaned back on the bench and stretched out his legs. "Yes, and that dates back from when we used to deliver papers together. We formed SJM ten years ago. And we've made a good team. But I think we're both ready now to strike out on our own."

Claire was about to ask him what he meant, when he looked at his watch and exclaimed sharply. "I've let the time get away from me. I've got to be back in Newton for a meeting in half an hour."

His mention of business reminded Claire of the purpose of their lunch. She had been so caught up in his casual recollections that she'd forgotten all about her reason for calling him in the first place. And she suspected he had too. "But we haven't even discussed Judge Turnbull," she pointed out now.

Spence stood up and offered her his hand. "Tell you what, why don't we continue the discussion over dinner tonight?"

Claire hesitated only a moment. "Yes," she agreed, letting him help her up. "I'd like that."

As the afternoon wore on, Claire found herself looking forward to the evening more and more eagerly. Feeling distinctly sheepish, she left the office early in order to give herself plenty of time to get ready.

You just saw the man at lunch. Stop acting like a teenager going out on her first date, she chided herself as she sat in the old-fashioned upholstered vanity chair by her bed, filing her nails and peering at her collection of nail polishes. This morning Spence had taken her by surprise. But this evening would be different, and she wanted to look her best. Would Spence like Moroccan Melon or Cloud-Lined Pink? she wondered, turning the bottles one by one in her fingers. She finally settled on the melon. It was slightly daring, and she felt that way tonight. As she sat letting the polish dry, she mentally went through the clothes in her closet. This time a tailored ensemble was definitely out, she decided at once. She didn't want to look businesslike tonight. She wanted to be feminine—and, yes, desirable.

When her polish was completely dry, she padded to the closet and pulled out the black jersey dress that she was always reluctant to wear because of its plunging back and clinging lines. It had been just the thing for New York cocktail parties but seemed a little much for Emerson Mills. Tonight, though, she felt reckless.

Holding up the dress in front of her slender body, she looked critically at herself in the full-length mirror. The blow dryer had made her dark hair frame her face in a soft wreath of dark curls. And her eyes looked startlingly blue beneath the arcs of her brows. Her excitement showed in her skin. Even without makeup it glowed with an inner warmth. *Is all this because Spence McCabe is taking me to dinner?* she asked herself wryly. *What's happening to me?*

But she dismissed the question. There was no point in asking it now. Her emotions were ruling her head, and no attempt at logical thinking was going to have the slightest effect. She wanted to see Spence again. And now that she had admitted that to herself, the matter was settled.

CHAPTER SEVEN

When Spence picked Claire up an hour later, her cerulean eyes were sparkling. His own eyes brightened when he took in her daring black dress and elegant beauty. Even the most obtuse of men would have been flattered by the special effort she'd made with her appearance tonight. And Spence was far from obtuse. As he stood at the foot of the stairs watching her go back up for the evening bag she had forgotten, his eyes caressed the sleek, curving lines of her body possessively. Even the gentle sway of her hips as she walked seemed to suggest that tonight would be special for both of them.

When Claire had called that day he'd almost kept the exchange on a strict business level. She'd been so angry with him before that he'd vowed not to make a fool of himself with her again. But the sound of her clear, feminine voice had weakened his resolve. And now he was glad that he'd been able to distract her from the subject of Turnbull at lunch so she would agree to dinner. Maybe at last they were going to come to an understanding. Fervently, he hoped so.

As Spence led Claire down the front steps she noted that the car waiting in her circular drive was not the ancient station wagon she had last seen full of lumber but a silver-gray LTD.

Her escort was amused as he saw her eyes widen. "I believe in the right transportation for the right occasion," he quipped. "And for taking a sexy beauty like you to dinner, something a little more elegant than Old Faithful is definitely in order."

"Old Faithful is your station wagon, I take it," Claire responded, settling into the plush burgundy upholstery.

He walked around to the other side of the car and opened the door. "Yes. It's an old family retainer and it does yeoman service. I not only use it to cart lumber, but it comes in handy for camping trips. I like to get out into the wilds to think every now and then."

Yes, Claire mused as Spence inserted the key and turned on the powerful motor. Even though she now knew he'd grown up in a city, she could picture him in that sort of setting. He was the kind of man who would look good in a red plaid flannel shirt, tramping through the woods or heating a pot of coffee over an open fire.

The thought made her remember dinner. "Where are we going tonight?" she questioned, mentally running through the selection of local restaurants.

"To my place," he informed her.

She shot him a sideways look, but his expression gave nothing away as he looked for traffic before pulling out onto the main road.

"For dinner?" she asked, sounding a little startled. She had been looking forward to being with Spence tonight. But she had pictured them in a restaurant surrounded by other people. When she'd agreed to dinner after their companionable lunch by the river, she hadn't counted on such intimate surroundings so quickly.

"Afraid of my cooking?" he questioned, slanting her a teasing glance.

His cooking wasn't what she feared. But she didn't want to admit that now.

Spence kept the conversation light as he guided the big sedan toward Newton. It always startled Claire to drive down Emerson Pike and discover anew that what had once been night-darkened farmland was now ablaze with the lights of a thriving community. The construction of the new city had all happened so quickly that old-time county residents like herself still weren't used to the transfiguration.

"How do you like living in this place?" she asked, unconsciously letting an edge of irritation show in her voice.

"Do I detect disapproval?" Spence wanted to know, turning toward her for a moment as they pulled up at a stop sign.

Claire paused, trying to frame her reply in a way that would convey her feelings about Newton without being offensive. "You have to understand that I can't help but think of Newton as a threat to the kind of future I was telling you about this afternoon," she began. "When I grew up this was a rural community with rolling hills and tree-covered stream valleys. You know those manmade lakes everybody in Newton is so proud of?"

Spence nodded.

"Well, they're flooded pastureland. I can't help being like most of the people who have roots here. Even though we know 'progress' is inevitable, we're having trouble accepting the changes that have taken place."

Spence took her remark seriously. As he shifted into first gear, his thick brows furrowed thoughtfully. For a moment he seemed to be concentrating on his driving, looking out the windshield without replying. "I see what you mean," he finally said, almost startling her. "All of this instant development would be pretty unsettling if you'd gotten used to being out in the country. But there's a lot you can say in Newton's favor. It's been carefully planned. And as cities go, it's damned successful. The architecture is award-winning. And the developers have done their best to preserve—and even enhance—the natural beauty of the setting." As he spoke he gestured toward a handsome complex of medical offices, artfully nestled in a stand of mature oaks and maples. There was no doubt the buildings had been carefully sited to take advantage of the natural terrain. "This is no ticky-tacky development," Spence continued. "It's something innovative and exciting in city planning."

Claire admitted that Spence had a point. As the big silver car cruised past the downtown shopping area with its attractive low-rise buildings and futuristic glass-enclosed shopping mall, she allowed herself to see the urban landscape with less prejudiced eyes.

"You know, there are people living in the county who always go into Baltimore to shop because they hate Newton so much," Claire revealed with a chuckle.

Spence shot her a surprised look. "I hope your prejudices aren't as strong," he declared, turning off the boulevard onto a curving residential street. It was lined with attractive contemporary white stucco town houses. In the next moment he was pulling the LTD into a short driveway beside the aging station wagon Claire remembered from before.

"Is this where you live?" she asked, looking up to admire the clean lines of the two-story structure. She had been to a party not long ago on this court and knew that the houses backed onto the lake. One of Spence's neighbors was a newly elected U.S. Congressman and another the head of the local school board.

"Yes," Spence conceded, getting out of his side of the car and coming around to hers. "I could have rented something bigger, but I decided to buy and this property was a bargain. The former owners had a Labrador retriever that tore the place apart. I've spent a lot of my spare time just replacing the doorjambs and the parquet floors."

The front door of the dwelling was sheltered from the street by a charming, brick-paved courtyard lined with planters and just now carpeted with dull-gold autumn leaves from the surrounding trees.

"Sorry I didn't have time to sweep here." Spence apologized for the leaves as he opened the door and showed Claire into a rather starkly plain foyer. But when she entered the living room she could see that he really had been hard at work. The floor had been newly covered with rich dark oak strips in a herringbone pattern. The soft gray of the walls was set off by a few clean-lined contemporary paintings. At one end of the room a carpeted dining platform was a dramatic focal point.

"I'm glad I got that finished last weekend," he told Claire, gesturing at the impressive structure holding a chrome and glass dining room set over which hung a softly lit smoked lucite chandelier. "Otherwise we'd be eating in the kitchen."

"I wouldn't have minded," Claire murmured agreeably.

"I would have," he returned, his green and dark gold gaze lingering appreciatively on the elegant lines of her jersey dress. "A beautiful woman deserves the proper setting," he went on, looking directly into her blue eyes. "And you are a very beautiful woman."

Claire felt her cheeks go warm. Embarrassed by his compliment, she turned away to admire the furniture in the living room. All of it was in proportion to the man who owned it. The maroon velvet couch was comfortably outsize. And the matching easy chairs looked like she could curl up in them and fall asleep.

"Would you like a drink?" Spence inquired, moving across the room toward a handsome sideboard which Claire realized was a liquor cabinet. It didn't look like anything she'd ever seen in a furniture store.

"You didn't make that too?" she asked.

As he opened one of the tambour doors to reveal a wet bar, Spence shot her a gratified look. "Yes, I did. When I moved here I gave all my old furniture to my brother and his wife. They'd just moved into a big house full of empty rooms, so they really appreciated my stuff. And that gave me a chance to start fresh in my new home. The sideboard is one of my more ambitious projects."

"Well, the results are fantastic," Claire complimented him. "If you ever want to give up the newspaper business, you could make a living as a cabinetmaker." And it was true, she mused. Spence was obviously quite an accomplished craftsman. Those large hands of his were capable of very delicate work. And she flushed anew, realizing where her errant thoughts were leading. She was remembering how his hands had once aroused her to heights of passion she'd never before experienced. Could they do that to her again? she wondered, and knew the answer was yes.

"What would you like to drink?" he inquired, unaware of the sensuous turn her thoughts had taken. She was thankful his broad back was to her as he searched through the impressive array of bottles.

A dry martini, she started to reply and then remembered how she'd downed more than one of those lethal cocktails that first evening when she and Spence had made love. Maybe she should choose a less potent drink. "White wine would be fine, if you have it."

Spence directed an amused glance at her over his shoulder. "Coming right up." It was as though he had read her mind and was humoring her, she reflected, eyeing the seating arrangement in the living room. She would be better off avoiding the capacious sofa. A few minutes later Claire nestled on one of the outsize chairs while Spence sprawled on the couch with a Scotch on the rocks between his large fingers. The curtains on the tall sliding glass doors leading to the balcony hadn't been drawn, and through them Claire could see one of the lakes she'd mentioned on the drive into town. In her present mood the setting was both peaceful and romantic. That combined with the soft mood music Spence had switched on made it difficult for Claire to introduce the subject that had been the excuse for coming here.

Judge Turnbull could wait till after dinner, she decided. Thoughts of their meal made her curious. "When are you going to start cooking?" she asked lightly as she sipped at her Chablis.

"Our food is in the oven staying warm," Spence admitted, with a rueful grin. "I can handle the basics like scrambled eggs and steak, but I thought something a bit classier was called for tonight, so I had it catered."

"You didn't have to go to a lot of trouble on my account," she protested.

A faintly amused smile quirked the corners of Spence's mobile lips. "Believe me, calling a caterer was a lot less trouble than doing it myself. And besides," he added, tossing her another one of his direct looks, "this is a special occasion for me and I felt like celebrating." When Claire's expression became puzzled, he went on to explain. "This is the first time you've really agreed to be with me since I arrived in town, and it means a lot. We both know that press conference with Bert Patterson and lunch this afternoon didn't count."

Claire was still dwelling on the meaning of those words when Spence suggested a few minutes later that they begin dinner.

"Anything I can do to help?" she inquired, following him as he moved with his gracefully controlled stride through the dining room to the kitchen.

Spence turned toward her with that half smile again. "If I'd known you were going to be so compliant, I would have let you set the table. But since I've already done that, how about bringing in the salad and dressing it. The bowl is in the refrigerator, and you'll find oil and vinegar in the pantry."

Compliant? Did his choice of words have another hidden meaning for her to reflect on? she wondered as she opened the refrigerator. Or was it her own unruly mind that was running along this suggestive track?

"What is that wonderful aroma?" Claire asked as Spence extracted a covered dish from the oven.

"You're just going to have to wait to find out," he teased, setting it on the stove top and rummaging in the drawer for a trivet.

He had taken off his jacket and draped it over a kitchen chair and she could see the play of firm muscles under the fine cotton of his striped shirt. As he straightened she moved away. But the kitchen was small, and when Claire turned back from the pantry with the dressing cruets, she almost collided with Spence. Putting his large hands on her shoulders, he murmured, "Steady, there," into her ear. At the contact with his solid masculine body she felt a shiver of remembered excitement course through her veins. Steady, indeed, she warned herself. Just what was all this leading to? she wondered. But she wasn't yet ready to think about the consequences of this intimate little dinner date.

A few minutes later Claire and Spence sat down to a spicy dinner of Indian curry, white rice with raisins and almonds, and an assortment of condiments.

"I would have taken you for a steak-and-potatoes man," Claire exclaimed, eyeing the array of chutney, chopped peanuts, coconut, and crumbled bacon.

Spence chuckled as he spooned portions of the condiments onto his plate and then added the curry. "Appearances can be deceiving."

That was indeed true, Claire thought as she took a bite of the curry and found her eyes watering. Reaching for her wineglass, she took a generous swallow. "I think I'm going to need a glass of water," she gasped.

Spence grinned. "Try using the condiments. They really do help. But I'll get your water," he added, getting up and disappearing into the kitchen. A moment later he emerged with a large tumbler. "I should have thought to put water on the table, but I'm a seasoned curry aficionado and my taste buds were acclimated long ago."

Proving his claim, he began to eat with gusto. Claire, on the other hand, was much more cautious with her fiery dinner. It was quite good though, she discovered after the first shock—the kind of thing she might have expected to find in New York, but not so close to home.

"I didn't know Newton had an Indian restaurant," she remarked.

"Then you're not reading your press releases. That's how I found out about the Taj Mahal. It just set up business down by Lake Windsor last month."

"Touché," Claire acknowledged, taking a small sip of wine.

"But I see you are interested in the number of Newton restaurants that have been closed by the health department lately," he added with a grin.

She looked up in surprise. It was true that in an acerbic mood she had written a rather nasty editorial on the topic —but that had been months ago. Had Spence been doing the same as she and digging up back numbers of the *Gazette* to read her comments on local issues?

Spence seemed to read her mind. "I've given myself away, haven't I? Reading your editorials has been a way of getting to know you better when you wouldn't let me take you out."

Claire was touched. Somehow the admission cast a new light on their relationship. And she realized suddenly that she had been hoping he was reading her words, just as she had been reading his. In fact, during the last weeks as she sat at her typewriter she'd actually been thinking of him when she labored over her weekly commentary.

"I've been reading you too," she admitted shyly. "So now we're even. And you're right; it's been a way of getting to know you better. And there have been some questions I've been wanting to ask you." The conversation turned easily to some of their mutual concerns. And once again Claire found that she could be comfortable with Spence in a way that she couldn't remember being with any other man. They really did have a lot in common, she reflected as they talked companionably about the latest musical at the Mechanic Theatre in Baltimore.

She was only on her second glass when they finished dinner. And when Spence suggested Irish coffee, she agreed, telling herself that she'd been more than circumspect in her drinking tonight. But, as she soon discovered, it wasn't the wine that was having an intoxicating effect on her.

After they cleared away the dishes and left the dining room, Spence turned the lights low and closed the drapes before guiding her to the broad couch. Soft music from the stereo filled the room with gentle, romantic sound.

"We have to talk about Judge Turnbull," Claire murmured as he slid his arm around her shoulder.

"No, we don't. He's all yours," Spence corrected. "We have better things to do."

"Better things?" She looked up into his eyes. They glowed darkly down at her. And in the subdued light their depths seemed almost mysterious. But there was nothing unfathomable about what was happening between her and Spence again tonight, Claire knew. All during their meal, even when they had been talking about local politics and personalities, there had been an electric sexual tension between them, and now it was humming almost audibly in the dimly lit space. In the darkened room the shadows shrouded the strong planes of his face, but he was not being secretive about wanting her tonight. She could feel his desire reaching out to her tangibly, coiling around her like a seductive web. It was there in the tone of his deep voice, the way his eyes dwelled on her face, the touch of his hand as his fingers slowly kneaded the soft material covering her shoulder. And she could feel herself responding to that need with desire of her own. She had been responding from the moment she'd heard his deep voice on the phone earlier today. How was this evening going to end? she asked herself yet again. Surely if she was wise she would leave now. But where Spence McCabe was concerned, she had never been wise.

Claire turned her head away from his and sipped at the strong brew in the tall cup she held, intensely aware of his arm resting lightly along her shoulder and the warmth of his body so close to hers.

"What are you thinking?" he asked, his grip tightening slightly.

"Nothing much. Just enjoying sitting here quietly."

Spence looked down at the top of her head. "With me?"

Claire nodded slowly. Why deny the truth? "Yes, with you."

He heaved a small sigh of satisfaction. "I'll tell you what I'm thinking . . ."

Claire looked up a bit apprehensively. "Yes?"

Spence smiled slowly, the movement of his well-shaped mouth deeply attractive to her. "I was remembering how we danced together back at that hotel. That was the first time I got to hold you in my arms, and it meant more to me than I can tell you." He paused, studying her face intently. "Would you dance again with me?"

"Now?" she asked, distressed to hear that her voice quavered slightly.

He nodded and his hand moved to the back of her head, stroking the smooth dark hair lightly. "Now."

Claire swallowed. She knew that if she agreed, she would be offering Spence more than a dance. But she couldn't say no. She wanted to be held in his arms, to feel their warm strength around her. "Yes."

The simple agreement seemed to echo in the room like

a momentous decision. Spence's hand paused on her head. And then suddenly he was standing before Claire, holding out his arms. She sat very still, looking helplessly up at him. Once again doubts about what she was doing assailed her.

"Maybe we shouldn't . . ." she began.

But in the next instant her host stepped forward and wrapped his sinewy fingers lightly around her arm. Before she could finish her weak protest he had pulled her to her feet and hauled her close to the lean muscularity of his large body.

"What are you afraid of?" he whispered gruffly into her ear. "Are you afraid of me? But you must know that I wouldn't do you any harm, Claire. For months now I've been aching for you, dreaming of you. I want to make love to you, not hurt you."

She could say nothing. Her tongue seemed glued to the roof of her mouth. She could only bury her face in his shoulder and drink in his heady essence.

Folding her tightly in his arms, his body began to sway gently to the music and Claire's automatically moved in harmony. She too had been wanting this closeness, and now that she was in the warm strong haven he offered, she could not have broken free if her life depended on it. She knew where this was going, but she was too busy drinking in the heady wonder of Spence's body moving against hers to heed any more half-hearted warnings. For weeks now she had been fighting herself and him, but now all the fight was gone from her. Like a sleep-drugged child, she lay against Spence's frame, letting him guide her in the small, darkened living room.

Shadows flickered around them, sealing them off in a tiny, private world of their own. The music seemed to flow on endlessly. Against her legs Claire could feel the solidity of Spence's thighs rubbing seductively. She stirred in restless anticipation. Spence's arms tightened around her and she succumbed quickly to the insistent pressure, no longer able to resist this heavenly sweetness. There would be no more denials tonight, she acknowledged. The need flaring to pulsing life between her and this man was too potent to push back.

Spence's hand had moved from her shoulder blades to the back of her neck where he began to stroke the sculpted hollow at her nape. His cheek, now faintly prickly, was resting on the top of her head. Moving, he nibbled for a tantalizing moment on her ear, his tongue darting out to explore the outer recess.

Claire shivered at the sensation this produced, but made no protest. Encouraged, Spence's mouth slid down to the side of her cheek to explore the length of her neck. When she moaned softly, his hand tipped back her head so that he could kiss her lips. At the same time his other hand curled around the soft flesh of her buttock and pressed her against the cradle of his own hips so that she could feel the burning imprint of his masculinity. When she gasped her awareness, Spence's tongue began to plunder her mouth more deeply. One hand held her head to his while the other joined their hips. Caught in this erotic trap, the two of them circled slowly to the music.

"This feels so good," he growled in a dangerous jungle purr. "Do you have any idea how good this feels? Don't stop me, Claire. I want you so badly tonight that I don't think I can stand it if you stop me."

For an answer she looked up into his face, her blue gaze seeming to melt into the hot, dark fires of his. She said nothing, but no words needed to be spoken. Her acquiescence was plain for him to read.

When Spence's hands finally left her head and hips, they moved softly down her neck and shoulders to the gentle swell of her breasts. Carefully, he outlined their shape, his thumbs circling her softness until the delicate peaks stiffened. When he felt her response, his left hand slipped inside the jersey material at the back of her low-cut dress and unhooked her bra. In the next instant he was sliding the zipper of her dress down to her waist so that her upper body was completely vulnerable. She shivered with excitement, waiting for what must happen next.

As they continued to sway together, Claire was blazingly aware of his hands on her naked breasts. With infinite care he weighed them in his palms and then traced delicious random patterns around their taut nipples. And then he was opening the buttons of his shirt so that he could press his masculine, hair-thatched chest to her softness. Claire shuddered with response. Up till now she had been passive, merely letting him make love to her while she submitted mindlessly. Now she broke free. She wanted this man, she told herself fiercely, and tonight she would have him regardless of what the morning might bring.

Claire's hands went to Spence's buttocks, kneading the solid flesh there in undisguised eagerness as she arched against him. When her breasts were crushed to his chest, a convulsive tremor ran through his taut body. His tongue left her mouth and his lips settled hot over her ear.

"Temptress! Can you feel what you're doing to me? Can you feel how much I want you?"

"Yes," Claire whispered back. She could feel his rising, surging desire and the knowledge of her power over him was an added intoxication.

Spence's hands lowered to her waist and she felt him tug at her dress. In the next instant it was on the floor, a pool of jersey at her feet. And she was standing in nothing but her lacy, French-cut black panties.

He stood away from her a moment, his eyes taking in her all-but-naked body hungrily.

"You're so beautiful, Claire." Abruptly, he pulled her close again and began dropping fiery kisses on the smooth line of her jaw and then her throat. Lifting her off the floor in a sudden convulsive gesture, he buried his face in her throbbing breasts, tasting first one nipple and then the other until her flesh seemed to glow. Claire trembled in the powerful vise of his arms. Hot fires were beginning to explode within her. They found a simmering focus as Spence shifted his attentions lower. With slow seduction his hard fingers slipped beneath the elastic of her panties and began to fondle with languorous stroking motions the hidden secrets of her femininity. Claire's sharp intake of breath told him all he needed to know. Slowly, sensuously, his hand fanned the burgeoning conflagration that threatened to consume her.

"Spence," she gasped. "Please, I can't stand it!" Her own hands fluttered and danced over the surface of his arms and shoulders and then began to tug in unfettered impatience at the closure of his waistband.

"In time, love," he whispered thickly in her ear. "Everything in time."

Guiding her to the couch, he stretched her out so that once more she lay almost completely naked before his scorching gaze. His darkened eyes caressed her breasts. And then, as he knelt beside her, his lips and tongue caressed her as well, closing over the hardened rosy peaks to suckle a sweetly tormenting path. And as his mouth excited her, so did his hands. Once again they slipped beneath her panties to explore with growing boldness the damp warmth he found there.

Claire tautened, going rigid as her desire for him built unendurably. Recognizing the height of her arousal, Spence slipped off her panties. When she was entirely free of them, his questing mouth investigated the soft flesh of her stomach and thighs, moving with sure demand.

Claire gasped and cried out, her hands twisting feverishly in his hair. When he levered himself up to unzip and discard his own slacks, it seemed like an eternity before he returned to Claire's taut body. His knee parted hers and he settled himself between her quivering legs.

Looking down into her glowing eyes, he took her face between his hands and forced her to meet his steamy gaze.

"Tell me you want me, Claire," he whispered in a thickened voice. "I want to hear the words from you. I need to hear them."

"Oh, yes, Spence! Oh, yes! I want you very badly!" Convulsively, her arms wrapped around his neck, drawing him closer. At the same time her hips arched up against his, signaling her feminine need. She could feel him pressed against her thigh, hard and firm.

Her spoken acknowledgment seemed to spur him. Seizing her silken buttocks, he guided himself into the quivering, molten softness that yearned to receive him. Claire gasped as he filled the aching emptiness. And then their bodies were joined completely. For a moment he was still, and together they savored the feeling of oneness. But Claire could not long be content with this passive union. Restlessly, her hips began to strain beneath the hard weight of his large, solid frame. In response, his hands tightened on her waist, pressing her into himself. The movement seemed to fill her even more totally, and she moaned aloud at the sensation. Unconsciously, her hands moved up and down his back, sensing with delight the hard bone and powerful sinew they found.

And then, slowly, Spence began to move within her. Even though his actions were careful and deliberate, each timed plunge sent high-pitched shivers rippling like shock waves through her system. She wriggled beneath him, unable to bear the controlled pace he was setting. But he was adamant, refusing to be affected by her attempts to increase the rhythm of his lovemaking. Claire was at his mercy as he built the tension within her to a tight, aching fist of urgency.

"Oh, Spence, please," she moaned. It was then that he began to thrust with overwhelming force. She was lifted higher and higher. And then suddenly she experienced an explosion of sensation. Her whole body seemed incandescent with indescribable feelings. Claire cried out as she acknowledged her ecstasy, and Spence's hands tightened on her body as he felt and heard it. But he didn't stop. And before the first incredible sensations had died from her loins, they were rekindled again, lifting her to even greater heights of ecstasy. It was only after that that Spence took his own pleasure, arching his powerful back in joy and release.

When it was over they lay pressed together for a very long time. Finally, Spence lifted his head and looked down into Claire's eyes. She gazed back lovingly. With a sense of wonder she took in the details of his face. As though rediscovering him, she savored the faint lines around his eyes and the proud thrust of his nose. There were grooves at the sides of his mouth—marks of the unhappiness he had seen in his life? Raising herself, she kissed each one tenderly. Spence smiled and the questioning look in his eyes softened.

"Stay the night with me, Claire. Let me carry you to my bed."

"Yes," she agreed simply. There was no thought in her head of wanting to go. When he left her body and stood to scoop her up into his arms, she felt she was home.

CHAPTER EIGHT

The sound of migrating Canada geese squawking as they landed on the lake outside the bedroom window awoke Claire. She was disoriented for only a brief moment while she blinked in the sunlight streaming over the bed. Then she realized where she was. Her blue eyes stared blankly at the ceiling. Once more she'd spent the night with Spence McCabe. And though this time she'd been perfectly sober, still she hadn't stopped to think of the consequences. She'd responded to his sexual magnetism like a compass needle pointing north. And as she turned her head to look over at the strong profile of his sleeping face, she was still undeniably drawn to him. After the ecstasy of their explosive lovemaking last night, how could it be any different? Even now those memories were kindling an aching warmth in the haven he had possessed so completely. She remembered how he had carried her upstairs to his bedroom and laid her on the brown velvet quilt that now covered her nakedness. And then his body had been pressed to hers as he rained kisses on her forehead, her eyelids, her temples, her cheeks, and her passion-swollen breasts. Once again they had been consumed by the ardor that had inflamed them earlier. Claire closed her eyes, remembering that vivid, aching sweetness. But it was over now. Now must come the inevitable reckoning.

It was time, she told herself sternly, for her head to rule her emotions. Spence McCabe was a business rival. He might want her, but he also wanted her paper. Was this his way of getting to it? Because he certainly had gotten to her last night. She had melted in his hands like butter in a hot frying pan. And now she had better leave before she did something foolish all over again.

When Claire turned with the intention of inching toward the edge of the outsize bed, however, she got a surprise. Something tightened around her ankle. And all at once the sleeping man beside her came fully awake. In an instant Spence's hair-rough arm was around her, pinning her naked shoulders to the mattress. She was engulfed by a dizzying mix of sensations—the feel of hard, masculine flesh, his clean male scent, the aura of strength and purpose that always seemed to emanate from him, and then his deep, gravelly voice.

"I thought you might try that disappearing act again," he growled laughingly into her ear before he nuzzled it with his lips. "Well, this time I made sure I wouldn't wake up to find you gone." He moved his leg and Claire's jerked along with it.

They were tied together at the ankle by some soft material. Without releasing her shoulder, Spence drew his leg up, forcing her to follow suit. She began to wriggle in protest, but he only shot her an amused grin while his powerful hand pressed her down into the bedclothes. In the next instant his tousled head disappeared beneath the covers. Claire watched in amazed consternation as the bed's quilt heaved and shifted above his body. When she felt his hands brush slowly across her naked hips, she couldn't stop herself from squeaking in protest. Tantalizingly, his touch ran downward along the line of her thighs, then under her knees and along her calves until it stopped to linger on her right ankle. "Spence, what in the world . . ." she objected weakly. But his intentions soon made themselves plain as she felt his deft fingers untie whatever bound them together. A moment later he reemerged, grinning broadly and waving an out-of-style wide silk tie. "I knew this thing would come in handy for something if I saved it long enough," he crowed.

Claire stared at him open-mouthed. "What . . ." she began to sputter. But he only silenced her with a brief kiss. "I wasn't going to wake up with you gone again, woman! So, after you fell asleep, I decided to make sure you'd stick around for the second act."

"What second act?" she questioned, beginning to feel sensations of alarm mixed with excitement course through her veins.

"This one," he retorted as his lips found hers once more and his body crushed hers beneath his.

"Spence, I have to get to work," she protested breathlessly when his mouth finally rose.

But he only shook his head and grinned with devilish willfulness. "No, you don't," he told her. "You're the boss and so am I. Authority has its privileges." Shifting his weight, he reached for the bedside phone and handed it to her. "Now call your honcho Vicchio, and tell him you're having trouble getting out of bed and won't be in until afternoon."

"If you expect me to do that, you're crazy," Claire sputtered.

"No, I'm not crazy," Spence informed her, lowering his

mouth to her breast and nibbling sensually on the rosy nipple that began to tauten at his knowing touch.

"You're impossible," Claire murmured, feeling her voice thicken with desire. She would never be able to talk to someone who knew her as well as Joe in her condition. Hastily she dialed the *Gazette*'s receptionist and left a message.

When she had finished, Spence lifted the receiver from her hand and replaced the phone on the night table. "Now, where were we," he growled, pulling her into his brawny arms.

Claire felt her body melt against his. And once more she was caught in the circle of magic that only Spence could draw around her. She felt the circle contracting into an enchanted world that included only the two of them. And when it had finally burst into a shivering glory that left them both breathless and wholly satisfied, Spence rolled on his side and pressed her head to the curve of his hard shoulder.

"We're very special together, Claire," he whispered lovingly into her ear. "I don't want you ever to try to sneak out of my bed again. That is," he amended with a chuckle, "unless you take me along." His hand stroked down the length of her back, and she almost purred with pleasure at the touch. But then Spence broke the sensual spell. "Right now I suggest we both take a short trip to the shower." Throwing back the cover, he rolled away, scooped her up in his arms, and strode across the room. Away from the warmth of the quilt, Claire shivered slightly and then nestled against the warmth of his chest. As he moved she caught a brief glimpse of their naked bodies in the mirror on the closet door. The contrast was startling. Her slim white form cradled so easily in his oak-hard arms looked fragile. The perfect foil to his tall, sturdy magnificence. And he was, she thought, looking up at the firm line of his jaw, a truly magnificent man—the kind of man that a woman runs across once in a lifetime. If she's lucky, Claire added to herself a trifle smugly. For right at that moment she felt like a very lucky woman indeed. Spence had swept away her foolish morning-after doubts. Now there was no question in her mind that she and this man were meant for each other.

That conviction was considerably strengthened under the warm running water of Spence McCabe's luxurious white composition marble shower. Setting her down gently in the enclosure, Spence ran his hands possessively over the elegant line of her back and then drew her close to the shelter of his body and let the warm water spill luxuriously over their entwined limbs. After the nip of cool morning air in the bedroom, the heat of the water was another sensual delight to Claire. And Spence obviously felt the same way.

"This could get to be a habit," he told her, rich laughter in his voice. "If we lived together, we'd never get to our offices. But maybe it would be worth the risk," he added after a brief pause, tipping her head up and brushing spiky strands of wet hair from her eyes.

The idea of living with Spence was suddenly immensely appealing. She could just imagine intimate little dinners like the one last night, days spent in his company, and nights being held in his arms. Was he asking her to live with him? she wondered as she watched him rub soap between his palms. And if he ever did come right out and ask her, what would she answer? She knew what she wanted her answer to be. But the rational part of her mind warned her that was impossible. When he had worked up a frothy lather, he began to soap her body with surprisingly delicate care. Lovingly, his hands ran over the curves of her shoulders and breasts and then down across the flat plain of her belly to the soft flesh of her thighs. And when he was finished, she did the same for him, marveling all the while at the rippling interplay of muscle beneath her questing fingers.

"How do you keep in such fantastic shape?" she questioned. "You have the body of an Olympic athlete."

Spence laughed, but he looked pleased. "I jog in the morning and work out with weights at the local health club," he informed her.

"Are you a fitness freak?"

"Maybe," he agreed. "I played football in college, and I got used to making exercise a regular part of my routine."

"Well, you didn't go jogging this morning," Claire countered, her blue eyes looking up at him teasingly from where she knelt in the shower stall.

"You have to take your exercise where you find it," he retorted, turning off the water and reaching for a towel. "And if a man only has one sport, maybe it should be . . ."

"Water skiing?" Claire asked ingenuously.

"Just what I was going to say," he agreed lustily, lifting her to her feet and kissing her soundly.

They toweled each other dry, and Claire giggled when he snapped the towel at her rear as she turned. "Is this what it's like to be in a men's locker room?" she questioned, enjoying the playful mood they had established.

"Not any of the locker rooms I've been in," Spence denied. "If it were, I'd still be in them."

Back in his bedroom, Spence pulled on jeans and a green turtleneck.

"What am I going to do?" Claire asked. "An evening dress is going to look ridiculous at ten A.M."

He paused in the doorway to shoot her a satisfied leer. "I like you the way you are now, but we don't want the neighbors to get the right idea," he added, ducking to elude the pillow she had hurled at his head. "Okay, okay," he placated her. "I'd offer you some jeans. But I'm sure they won't fit. Maybe we can smuggle you into your house in my raincoat. Meanwhile, for breakfast, why don't you wrap yourself in my bathrobe. It's on the hook in the closet. I'll go down and fix something for us to eat while you're getting ready."

Getting ready was only a matter of slipping her arms into Spence's terry-cloth wraparound and rolling up the sleeves so that they didn't hang over her hands.

Pulling on his robe made her feel as though Spence himself had pulled her into his arms. She could catch the masculine scent of his body in the rough fabric, mingled with the pungent tinge of his aftershave.

The robe suddenly made her feel possessive of the man. Spence was hers, she told herself. Maybe at one time he had belonged to another woman. But their lovemaking had surely made him hers. And now, for the first time, she could admit to herself that she was falling in love with him.

Tying the belt around her waist, she paused to look around at the room. Last night, and again this morning, Claire had been too caught up in the tumultuous emotions Spence's lovemaking evoked to pay any attention to her surroundings. But now she examined his private domain with curious eyes. As he had told her, all the furnishings were new and, like its owner, were supremely masculine. The curtains and bedspread were a chocolate brown. No rug adorned the floor. Its richly polished surface was a compliment to the wood of the other pieces in the sparsely furnished chamber. A handsome chest occupied the corner. A burgundy leather club chair was placed near the window. But the massive fourposter in which she had spent the night caught and held Claire's attention. It was clearly Spence's handiwork, and as she studied its handsome proportions and solid oak supports, a warm flush began to creep across her cheeks. The lingering tang of fresh varnish suggested he had just finished it. Had he crafted it with her in mind? she suddenly wondered. And would there be other nights in that welcoming bed? Abruptly, Claire headed out the door for the stairs with the idea of helping Spence in the kitchen.

But as she passed the small room at the end of the hall she caught a glimpse of a cluttered desk and bookcase stuffed haphazardly with books and magazines. *So that's how he keeps the rest of the house so neat. He shoves all the mess in here,* she told herself with a chuckle. Pausing, she was suddenly once more overcome by curiosity to see what must be his study and pushed the door farther open. Almost at once she wished she hadn't. Her eye was caught immediately by a large color photograph occupying a prominent position on the desk.

A cold feeling of dread gripped Claire as she moved closer in order to get a better look. The gold-framed picture had been taken at the beach and was a close-up shot of a man and a woman wearing bathing suits. The man was obviously a much younger Spence. But it was the woman he carried in his arms who riveted Claire's horrified gaze.

She was a slender, dark-haired beauty. *She looks a lot like me,* Claire thought, knowing she must finally be seeing a picture of Kathleen.

Suddenly another image was superimposed in her mind on the one she was looking at. Less than an hour before she had seen herself being carried in Spence's arms in almost exactly this way. With stiff, trembling fingers she picked up the photo and stared at it hard. Kathleen didn't really look like her, but they were the same physical type —dark-haired, slender, fairly tall. Kathleen's eyes had been brown, though, Claire realized with a touch of vanity, not blue like her own. But the expression on Kathleen's face was exactly the love-drugged look that had been on her own face earlier. And then her gaze shifted to the image of Spence. He was looking down at his wife protectively. Anyone could see at a glance that he was a man deeply in love. The expression on his face was one of pure adoration. It seemed to pierce Claire's heart like a knife.

With stiff fingers she set the picture back on the desk, being careful to replace it in the exact spot where it had previously rested. Like a zombie she turned back toward the door and left the room. The next thing she knew she was seated at the dining table, not able even to remember how she'd gotten downstairs. Sunlight spilled through the window onto the glass table in rich puddles of warm gold. But Claire felt cold. Shivering, she laced her hands together in her lap and stared down at the empty plate in front of her. Cold wasn't even the word for how she felt. Her insides were frozen, as though she'd suddenly been transformed from a woman in love to a lifeless ice sculpture.

Smiling broadly, Spence came in bearing a plate heaped with triangles of French toast. "This is one of my favorite breakfasts," he announced cheerfully. "But I don't often indulge myself. However, this *is* a special occasion." Ceremoniously, he forked three of the golden-brown wedges onto Claire's plate. She stared down at the food in silent misery. Even one bite would surely stick in her throat. Her hands began to tremble even more violently.

"Well, don't just sit there—dig in! You're supposed to smother that in maple syrup and then tell me what a fantastic cook I am," Spence prompted her as he doused his own serving with the thick, golden syrup.

He had already filled their coffee cups. In an effort to still her trembling hands and pull herself together, Claire reached for her steaming cup. But before she was able to bring it to her mouth, the hot liquid sloshed over the edge and drenched the pieces of toast on her plate.

"I said maple syrup, not coffee," Spence quipped. And then his voice trailed off as he took in the ashen pallor of her face.

He set his fork down. "My God, Claire, what's wrong? You look like you've seen a ghost."

It was a struggle to still the bubble of hysterical laughter trying to rise in her chest. Because what Spence had unwittingly said was exactly right. The ghost of Kathleen had come back to haunt her.

But instead of laughing, Claire confronted his puzzled look across the table and forced her voice into an impersonal conversational tone. "You know, Spence, I've thought a lot about what happened between us at that honeymoon hotel. I know why I was attracted to you, but I've always wondered what drew you to me." By sheer willpower she met his eyes steadily as she held her breath and waited for an answer.

But, uncharacteristically, Spence's gaze dropped from hers. "What kind of a question is that?" he hedged.

"You're a very beautiful woman. Any man would be attracted to you."

Claire drew in a deep shuddering breath. "Any man?" she asked. Despite her efforts at self-control, her voice had taken on a bitter edge. "Or do you mean any man who was still in love with his dead wife and thought I looked a lot like her?"

She stared at him challengingly, watching as the color drained from his face too. He sighed heavily. "Did you go into my office?" When she said nothing, he sighed again. "I suppose I should have put that picture in my office away. Obviously you've seen it and drawn all the wrong conclusions."

The numbed shock was wearing away, and anger was beginning to swarm through Claire's system. What Spence had done to her was unforgivable. He had deliberately used her. He had made her fall in love with him when all the time she was only a substitute for the woman he really wanted. The pain was so great Claire could hardly focus her eyes. "We both know why you didn't put that picture away. It's because you're still in love with her. And the reason you seduced me that night was because I look like her. I dare you to deny that!" Claire was now totally unable to control her voice. It had slid up to a hysterical pitch.

Spence pushed back his chair with a crash and stood up so that he towered over her. "All right, damn it, I won't deny that's what drew me to you. And I won't deny that I loved my wife—very much. When she died, I wanted to die too. But that was two years ago, Claire. I'm a different man now. And though there's a superficial physical resemblance between you and Kathleen, I hadn't talked to you five minutes before I found out you're a very different woman. I stuck around because I wanted to know you better. And whatever you think, that first night it was you I was making love to, not her."

Claire sat very still in her chair. "Then why," she asked with all the deadly calm she could muster, "did you call her name in your sleep?"

There was a long, painfully charged silence while Spence stared down at her. And then, abruptly, he turned his back and rammed his fists into his jeans pockets. "I don't know," he almost shouted. "Maybe I was saying good-bye."

Claire had had enough. She couldn't take any more of this. "Please take me home," she clipped out, rising to her feet.

"No!" Spence thundered. "If you want to go home, you'll have to walk there in that bathrobe. I'm going to keep you here until we clear this up. I was going to ask you to marry me this morning, Claire, and I can't just let you walk out of my life again!"

His words gave Claire's misery another point of focus. She was now completely over the edge. "Oh, you were, were you? Well, I know all about marriages like that. My father had a second wife, and I can tell you, Mr. Spencer McCabe, that she was never anything in his mind but a pale shadow of the woman he really loved. I'm not going to settle for something like that."

Spence came forward and took her by the shoulders. "Claire," he pleaded, his eyes boring down into hers, "you can't really believe that. I'm not your father, for God's sake. I'm the man who made love to you last night, who made love to you again this morning. Are you honestly going to call what we shared a pale shadow?"

Claire turned away. "I don't know what to call it. I only

know that I want to go home—now! And if you won't take me, then I'll call a cab. And my reputation be damned!" They stared at each other like duelists. But it seemed that, for the time being, she had fired the last shot.

"All right," Spence growled. "Go upstairs and put your clothes on. I'll take you home."

Neither Spence nor Claire spoke on the ride back to her house. She had put her evening dress on and sat in the passenger seat clutching his outsize raincoat around the sexy black jersey that now seemed like highly inappropriate funeral attire.

But when Spence pulled off the highway and into her drive, he did not head immediately for the big stone house. Instead, he stopped down the narrow lane and pulled off to the side under the giant oak trees.

Taking the key out of the ignition, he turned toward Claire, who bent her head away and tried to unlock the door. But Spence kept one hand firmly on the automatic door lock.

"I have something else to say to you. And you're going to sit here for another few minutes and listen," he rasped.

Claire was all ice now. "There's nothing you can say that I'd want to hear."

"Nevertheless, I'm going to say it. You don't know anything about my relationship with Kathleen. And, more to the point, it has nothing to do with you! I did love her. After she died I was like a dead man myself. For over a year life seemed like a pretty worthless endeavor. You don't know what an effort it was to bring myself back. It was only a few months before we met that I really began taking an interest in what was going on around me." Spence paused to run a weary hand through his brown hair. When he continued, his voice was thick with emotion. "Until I met you, Claire, I hadn't even thought about making love to another woman. You're the one who brought me all the way back to life. That first night, and then last night . . . Surely you can understand that I'm capable now of loving again."

His hand now gripped the steering wheel so hard that his knuckles showed white. "What's more," he continued doggedly, "you told me it wasn't so long ago that you were involved with another man. And yet, last night and this morning I'm certain you were responding only to me. God, was that important to me!"

Leaning forward, Spence grasped her shoulder so hard that it hurt. "Claire, let me tell you about Kathleen."

But Claire only shook her head. Caught up in a vise of pain, she'd hardly heard what he'd just said to her and had taken in none of its meaning. The name Kathleen jabbed at her, creating a fresh wound. She was too upset now to hear about his only love. It would tear her apart to hear him talk about his loving relationship with another woman.

"No, Spence," she whispered. "I couldn't take that now."

She watched him go pale as the remaining color drained out of his face. "I can't believe you just said that," he rasped. "If you're an adult, you'll admit that it's possible for a person to have more than one meaningful relationship in his or her life. I didn't know your father and I can't even guess at his motives in marrying your stepmother. But it's not fair to judge what I'm offering you by their marriage."

Claire was not capable of listening or responding rationally to Spence's logic. She could not hear the deep emotion in his voice. She could only feel her own agony of disillusionment. "How dare you accuse me of not being an adult," she flared suddenly, blindly striking out like a disappointed child, without considering her words. "You think that just because you're good in bed that I'm going to fall all over myself to sleep with you? Well, you're wrong. From now on, Spence McCabe, it's simply business between the two of us."

If possible, Spence's countenance went even whiter. There was a moment of leaden silence, and then his hand flipped the automatic lock, opening the doors. "What a fool I've been about you. You're not the person I thought you were at all," he grated, his voice dangerously quiet. And then he reached across and pushed open the door so that Claire could climb out.

Without a backward glance she did just that and began to stalk up the driveway, her shoulders hunched and her arms crossed tightly against her chest. Before she'd reached the door she heard the sound of his motor and the abrupt grate of wheels in her gravel drive as Spence backed up and sped away.

CHAPTER NINE

Shortly after the shattering scene in Spence's car, Claire learned from Joe that Judge Turnbull had called. The *Voice* had released him from his agreement, and he was ready and eager to be interviewed by a reporter from the *Gazette*.

"That's good news," Claire had remarked with forced cheerfulness.

"Yeah," Joe had agreed. "But I have some news that isn't so good. Joyce Rushing told me that Spence McCabe has flown back to Detroit to sign over managerial control of his midwestern interests to his brother, James. That means he's going to be concentrating all his efforts here. Of course Joyce is elated because she really goes for the guy. But it's bad news for us."

Claire tapped her fingers on her desk, not sure whether the surge of anxiety she felt was personal or professional. "Why? Don't you think we have what it takes to compete with the man?"

She had made the remark lightly, but Joe's response was dead serious. "I think if McCabe wants, he can run us off the tracks, Claire. He hasn't really tried to do it yet. Maybe something's been holding him back." Joe put a loafer-clad foot up on the low radiator beneath the window and looked out at the leafless trees pensively. "But the fact that he's making this kind of a move gives me the willies. There's almost something ominous about it."

Claire's chin rose. "Come on, Joe! You have too strong a tendency to see the dark side of everything, and right now you're sounding like the voice of doom."

But despite her pep talk to Joe, when the thin young man had left her office Claire's blue eyes were dark with worry. She and Spence hadn't exactly parted on good terms. It was the pre-Christmas advertising season, and there had been more than enough work at the paper to keep her mind occupied. In the past few days she had deliberately been refusing to think about the disastrous way their relationship had splintered to pieces. But now that Joe had brought up the subject of Spence McCabe, Claire was no longer able to banish his ruggedly handsome face from her mind. Sighing, she cupped her chin in her hands. For a few foolish hours she had let herself be lulled into thinking she could find happiness with him, but those hopes had been dashed. It had been the depth of her hurt that had made her say those hateful things to him in the car, she acknowledged. And now she wished some of those words could be taken back. She had accused him of seeing only Kathleen's shadow when he looked at her, and Claire still believed that was true. But she could no longer hold on to the anger she had felt earlier. It wasn't Spence's fault that she looked a little like his wife. And it wasn't Spence's fault that he'd tried to recapture the happiness he'd shared with Kathleen.

Suddenly, against her will, vivid memories of his lovemaking bubbled to the troubled surface of her mind. It had been both tender, and passionate and electrifying. Kathleen had been a lucky woman—in love, at any rate. *If only*

I'd met him first, Claire thought with another sigh, remembering how much they really did have in common —in and out of bed. Their thoughts on so many issues were the same. And sometimes it had even seemed as though they could read each other's minds. Pushing back her chair, she rose to her feet and began to pace the empty office. But she hadn't met him first. And she knew herself too well to believe she'd be able to accept second best with him now. Besides, she told herself bleakly, he'd left town the day after their little scene and hadn't been back since. Obviously, he wanted to avoid her. She wasn't going to get a chance to reconsider her painful decision. She had made her bed, she thought, laughing with bitter irony at the old cliché. So she might as well get on with the business of learning to lie in it—alone.

The cold gray weather that settled in with the first of December did nothing to lighten Claire's mood. And when Mandy came down from the attic hauling the box of elaborate decorations that were a Christmas tradition at Tanager Hall, Claire could enter into the work of hanging holly and tacking up mistletoe only half-heartedly. She felt badly in need of a distraction to keep her thoughts from Spence. Christmas with its reminders of family cheer and togetherness only heightened her feelings of unhappiness. And so she fell into a routine of swamping herself with work in order to come home from the office tired enough to simply eat dinner and then fall into bed and drop into a sleep of exhaustion.

The only small comfort she could take was that Spence was out of town—so that his weekly editorial was taken over by Joyce Rushing or someone else on the *Voice* staff. Claire was glad she didn't have to read Spence's own words now. They would have been too painful a reminder of the man himself—of how far away he was, both physically and emotionally.

Claire had settled into such a rut that when she picked up the phone in her office one Tuesday and heard Richard Buchanan's sophisticated New York tone on the other end of the line, it was like hearing a voice from another galaxy.

"Richard, is that really you?" she queried in astonishment.

"None other," he proclaimed, but she could hear the note of uncertainty in his voice. After all, he hadn't communicated with her since before his marriage, and he was probably wondering what sort of reception he would get from her. Claire smiled wryly at the receiver in her hand. Under normal circumstances, that reception would have been decidedly cold. But the circumstances since she'd read of Richard's marriage had been far from normal. The truth was that since meeting Spence she'd hardly given Richard a thought. And though she had every right to resent him, in fact she felt none of that emotion at all.

The romantic entanglement between them now seemed like ancient history. Hearing his voice was like bumping unexpectedly into an old friend. That and nothing more. And so when she answered, it was with a warmth that he had no right to expect.

"Where are you calling from?" she questioned cheerfully.

"Baltimore. We're doing a layout on Harborplace, and I decided to come down and supervise personally." He paused and then added hesitantly, "This is a quick trip, so I'm going back to New York tomorrow. Is there any chance you could join me for lunch at Phillips'?"

"Phillips'!" Claire exclaimed, picturing the wildly popular seafood restaurant that overlooked Baltimore's refurbished Inner Harbor. Its whimsical Victorian ambiance and eclectic collection of lifesize rag dolls and outrageously outré antiques never failed to lighten her mood. But time was always a problem at Phillips'. She glanced at her watch and frowned. "I can get away for lunch, but I can't afford to stand in a block-long line."

Richard chuckled with pleased surprise, as though he had only half-expected her to take him up on his invitation. "No problem. One of our photo sessions was at Phillips' and I'm getting the VIP treatment. They'll slip us in through the cocktail lounge."

Claire looked at the brown bag sitting on her desk. She'd packed herself a lunch for today, but now it held no appeal whatever. "I'll meet you at noon," she told Richard.

As she stopped by the washroom on her way out of the building, Claire examined her image in the mirror with more interest than she'd shown in days. Thank goodness she'd worn one of her favorite suits to the office today. But despite its rich cranberry color, she looked pale. Carefully she dusted on some blusher and touched up her lipstick. Though she was no longer interested in Richard romantically, she certainly didn't want him to think she'd been pining away on his account. No, she admitted to the slim, dark-haired image in the mirror. The pining she'd been engaged in lately had nothing whatever to do with Richard Buchanan.

As Claire hurried down the brick-lined quay, the scene at Baltimore's Inner Harbor was bright with life and color. The weather had changed for the better and scores of lunchtime shoppers were taking advantage of the crisp, clear afternoon. Gulls wheeled overhead, adding their hungry cries to the sound of cheerful voices. And the

December sun reflected brightly off the glass that enclosed the two elegant shopping malls that were the focal point of the harbor.

Phillips' dominated one whole end of the larger pavilion. And as Claire expected, a noontime line snaked all the way around a corner and hid the main entrance. But to her relief, Richard, as he had promised, was waiting at the door to the cocktail lounge. When he spotted her, his aristocratic features broke into an uncharacteristic grin of relief. Had he been thinking she might stand him up? she wondered with amusement. Well, maybe he deserved something like that. But Claire wasn't in the mood for revenge. You could only hate a man you felt strongly about, she realized with a little pang. And now all her deeper feelings were centered on Spence McCabe.

Dressed in an elegantly cut blue suit, Richard looked every inch the big-city magazine editor. He wasn't the type to get his hands dirty, Claire thought suddenly as he moved forward to greet her with a quick hug. He was completely unlike a certain small town newspaper publisher who liked to build things.

A moment later Richard was guiding her through the lounge into the dining room. The curving room was divided into small seating areas by a zany assortment of architectural elements like Victorian balustrades, stained glass windows, and gingerbread porches gleaned from mansions up and down the East Coast.

As they waited at a wrought iron table for their drinks, it was obvious to Claire that Richard wanted to say something to her, but was having trouble finding the words. Then, suddenly amused, it dawned on her what his predicament must be. It was so unlike him to be ill at ease in any situation that she was tempted to let him squirm.

But her better nature won out. Playfully, she decided to put him out of his misery and open the topic herself. "Well, how is married life treating you?" she asked with a guileless smile. "And by the way, I haven't had the chance to congratulate you." Inwardly, Claire couldn't help but be amazed all over again by her sense of detachment. Just a couple of months ago she had imagined herself in love with this man—the first news of his marriage had sent her reeling out of control. But now she felt nothing stronger than amused sympathy. Had her feeling for him been so shallow? Perhaps that was why she'd put their relationship in jeopardy in the first place. Maybe she'd never really been in love with him at all. God knows that if she'd felt for Richard what she now felt for Spence, she would never have risked losing the man by leaving him behind in New York.

However, she had never seen Richard look as uncomfortable as he did at that moment. And she began to feel sorry for him.

The publisher of America's fashion bible cleared his throat and fiddled with the cutlery on the table. "This meeting is long overdue, Claire. I owe you an apology," he finally forced out. "I know that when you found out about my marriage, you must have thought my behavior was inexcusable. In fact," he added, giving her a troubled look, "I expected you to hang up on me when I called today."

Neither of them noticed the arrival of the waiter, who unobtrusively put their drinks down on the table.

"I was too pleased to hear from you to hang up, Richard," Claire protested. "I hope we're still going to be friends."

Claire noted the smile of pure relief that spread across

Richard's regular features. Leaning forward, he went on in an earnest voice. "Claire, it all happened so quickly between Susanna and me. You've heard of women being swept off their feet. Well, I was swept off mine. Getting married was a very sudden decision, and somehow I couldn't bring myself to discuss it with you over the phone."

Claire had her own private interpretation for his statement. He hadn't had the guts to call her, he meant. But she wasn't going to say anything so uncharitable. She had decided that this luncheon was going to be an exercise in peace making.

But all the time she was ordering crab cakes and chatting with Richard, her mind was going through a reassessment process. She couldn't imagine Spence McCabe behaving as Richard had. He was too honest and straightforward a person to leave a woman twisting in the wind that way. And he was a stronger person, too, she added mentally.

By the end of lunch Claire and Richard were even talking amiably about his new wife. And Claire could tell by the glow in his voice that marriage was good for the man.

But when he asked about her life, she found herself talking a lot about the *Gazette* and Emerson Mills and not saying anything about what was really on her mind. There was no way she could tell Richard about Spence. How could you tell one man whom you'd muddled a love affair with about another with whom you'd just done the same thing? It would be funny if it weren't so plain awful, Claire thought, drawing patterns on the napkin with her fork as she chattered brightly about a new advertising campaign.

* * *

She didn't talk about Spence during lunch, but on the drive home she could no longer avoid the subject. All week she had been pushing him to the back of her mind. But now that was simply no longer possible. Like a suddenly uncaged tiger, his memory sprang at her and ripped all her defenses to shreds. It was the meeting with Richard, she realized, that had crystallized her feelings. He was just so different from Spence that she found it impossible not to make invidious comparisons. Richard was weak where Spence was strong, smoothly evasive where Spence was honest, shallow where Spence was capable of deep loyalty and commitment.

Spence was a hell of a man in just about every way. And with a sharp pang she began to fully realize what she would lose, might indeed already have lost, by rejecting his proposal. In her hurt and mortification, after seeing that loving picture of Spence and Kathleen, her reasons for breaking off their relationship had seemed to make iron-clad sense. But now those same reasons were beginning to melt like snow in the sun.

Once again the last scene between them in his car played itself through Claire's mind. He had told her that he cared for her. And he had wanted to tell her about Kathleen. But she had been too overwrought to listen. Suddenly her heart contracted as she began to understand what Spence had offered and what she had rejected. How callous he must think her! And he was right. She had been so wrapped up in her own emotions that she had been incapable of responding to his. Her cheeks flushed as her mind sped further back—to the way he had made love to her. He had practically worshipped her body, and that should have told her all she needed to know. He was right. She'd been out of her mind to draw analogies between her relationship with Spence and her father's with his second wife. Just the new furniture in his town house ought to have shown her how little they had in common. Spence had given away all those reminders of the past because he wanted to build a new life. Why couldn't she take Spence at his word and believe that he really did love her? But she knew why. Her father and her stepmother were just a convenient excuse. It was really her pride that had been damaged when she'd seen that picture of Spence and Kathleen on his desk. And now she was ashamed of her self-centered reaction. She had been thinking only of her own wounded feelings and not of Spence at all.

Claire's fingers gripped the steering wheel tightly. She knew now that she really wanted this man at any cost. She could only pray he still wanted her.

To Claire's astonishment, when she pulled into the drive of her house she saw Spence's car was parked in front. Her heart leaped when she saw it. She'd been wondering how she could apologize and tell him her real feelings. And now he'd made it easy by coming to her door.

But the smile of welcome on her face withered when she entered the living room. Spence was sprawled in an overstuffed chair. There was a brooding atmosphere in the room, and the expression on his face was anything but conducive to heartfelt confessions. It was tight with anger.

"Back at last from your rendezvous with your ex- or is it currently not-so-ex-lover?" he drawled insultingly.

Claire halted on the threshold and stared at him blankly. "What?"

"You heard me." Spence surged to his feet, his eyes raking her coldly. "I called your office this afternoon the first thing after getting back from Detroit. And they told me you were having lunch with Richard Buchanan. Well, I know all about you and Buchanan. He's the guy who ditched you that night I picked up the pieces." His voice was like chipped ice, rivaling the expression in his eyes.

Claire found herself taking a step backward. She'd been thinking warmly of him all during the drive home and wondering how to go about making peace. But the man who stood before her was completely unapproachable. She'd never seen Spence like this before. And for the first time she felt tremors of fear in his presence.

"You really had me fooled, Claire," he continued, his hand running over the back of a delicate antique parlor chair. "You look like a million dollars, and you surround yourself with only the best. And that's what I thought you were, too—the best. But you're not the lady you make yourself out to be. I don't know why I didn't see that our first night together. I thought you came to my bed because you felt something for me. But obviously I was just one in a line of lovers."

The cruel words flayed open barely healed wounds so that she gasped with almost physical pain. She had felt bad enough about her behavior that night. But to have Spence bring it up in this way was unbearable. She felt her whole body go rigid and cold as though she were standing in an icy wind.

"Spence, surely you don't really th-think . . ." She began to stammer. But he cut her off unfeelingly.

"I suppose you were avoiding me all that time because your sexual needs were still being taken care of by Richard." He spat out the name as though he hated it. "You probably only let me make love to you that night in my town house because he was unavailable. Apparently it doesn't bother you that he has a wife who's very much alive."

Claire sagged against the doorframe, her legs so rubbery that they could no longer hold her up.

Spence was still speaking, his words rumbling over her like soldiers marching over a grave. "And to think that I was such a fool that I severed my ties in the Midwest and moved my business to this area because of you. Oh, yes," he added, seeing the look of disbelief that transformed her face. "I had planned to expand to the East Coast, but it was only after I'd met you that I decided to start with Newton. I was following you, Claire. Because after that one night I wanted you back so much, nothing else seemed to matter. And after you turned down my offer, I could have crushed you and your antiquated operation as easily as I could this antique chair." His hand tightened on the delicate wood. And for a moment Claire half expected that he really would shatter it. But his fingers loosened again; and he straightened, his cold eyes never leaving her stricken face. "Well," he continued, "there's no reason to sit around twiddling my thumbs while I wait to win you over because I simply don't want you anymore. From now on, Claire Tanager, you're going to find out what the word *competition* means. I don't give you and the *Emerson Mills Gazette* three months." And with those parting words he brushed past Claire's sagging form and strode rapidly down the hall. The whole house reverberated as he slammed the front door behind him.

There was no longer any reason to hold back her tears. They came welling up in her eyes, literally blinding her as she staggered across the room to the couch and threw herself down. Misery seemed to engulf her like a shroud.

She knew now what it meant to be despised by Spence McCabe. And the feeling was crushing.

Tears coursed down Claire's cheeks and spilled onto the soft watered silk of the love seat. But she was oblivious to it. Everything was ruined now—her hopes for personal happiness and her ambitions for the *Gazette*. For she had no doubt that Spence meant exactly what he said. He had already driven her to her knees, and he was going to do the same to her paper.

CHAPTER TEN

Spence was wrong. It took less than two months for the *Voice* to have the *Gazette* on its knees.

Claire had little time to wonder where his attack would begin.

"Look at the way McCabe is undercutting our advertising rates," Joe huffed, charging into Claire's office without knocking and waving a printed sheet of paper in her face. "The bastard could ruin us with this price schedule."

Claire took the rate form and studied it silently, her brows knitting as she took in the meaning of the figures in front of her. "These rates wouldn't even cover our printing costs," she muttered, scanning the unbelievable figures one more time. "How can he afford to do it?"

"He can't. Oh, sure, his other papers can absorb the loss—temporarily, at least. But what I can't understand is why he's doing it now. I was prepared for something like this in the beginning. But when he held off, I figured we didn't have that much to worry about. It's like he's done a complete about-face." Joe scratched his head in perplexity, eyeing Claire as though she might have the answer.

She lowered her eyes. For a split-second she thought about giving Joe an edited version of the real story. But the very idea was just too painful. Instead, she hedged. "Maybe he was waiting to size up the situation here before he made his move."

Joe shook his head. "I don't know. I think that guy had the situation sized up from the beginning."

"Is there any way we can fight back?" Claire questioned.

"We just can't function with rates as low as that, Claire." Her news editor confirmed what she already knew. "In a showdown like this, we just have to rely on the loyalty of the county."

But when it came to dollar signs, loyalty turned out to be in short supply. Claire found her advertising base slipping away like sand undercut by a rising tide. Even her oldest clients cut their ad space in the *Gazette* and gave most of their business to the *Voice*. Since this was the Christmas season, when the *Gazette* traditionally fattened itself up for the lean beginning of the year, the loss was particularly devastating.

And if that wasn't bad enough, the *Voice* attacked on other fronts as well. With free trial subscriptions they began to entice county residents to try their wares. And to turn these new patrons into paying customers, they ran slick photo spreads and extended their coverage of county events. Spence took on extra staff and even moved up his publication day so that local events would automatically be reported in his paper first. For Claire it was a vicious cycle. New subscribers meant a larger circulation base for the *Voice*, which, along with the low rates, drew more advertisers.

Claire tried to fight back. She began by speaking to a few businessmen whom she knew personally. All were embarrassed and apologetic. But they shook their heads and pointed to their own lowered sales figures.

"These are tough times for everyone, Claire," one Main Street shop owner told her. "I wish I could ignore the *Voice*'s bargain rates. But with their new readers and circulation figures, an ad in their paper means I'm reaching not only the people in Newton, but my old customers in the county too."

There was nothing more Claire could say. Pulling up her collar against the bitter December wind that moaned between the gray stone buildings of the old mill town, she trudged back toward her office. Emerson Mills had always been "her" town. Merchants had always greeted her on the street, and many had even come out of their shops to chat for a moment. But now she found herself being ignored and even avoided. She tried to tell herself it was nothing personal. These people didn't think about the consequences of succumbing to Spence's siren song. Times were tough and they had their own businesses to look out for. Still, it hurt to find out how shallow their loyalty did run when their pocketbooks were affected.

The realization was brought home even more in January.

"Can I talk to you?" Joe Vicchio asked, an uncharacteristically uncomfortable expression on his mobile face. He looked like he had bad news, and Claire steeled herself for more reports of ad revenues lost and news stories scooped.

But, if possible, what Joe had to say was a worse blow. After closing the door to her office, he slowly pulled up a chair in front of her desk as if trying to postpone the reason for his visit as long as possible.

Then, taking a deep breath, he plunged ahead. "I hate

to tell you this right now, Claire. I know this is a bad time for you. And I feel like a rat . . ."

"Well, get it over with," she prompted, wondering what could possibly be causing him so much discomfort. Joe was not usually the type to mince words.

"Okay. *The Baltimore Sun* has offered me a job on their news staff. And I've decided to take it."

Claire certainly hadn't been prepared for that. She'd known of course that Joe was too talented to be satisfied with a job on a small paper forever. But she hadn't thought that he was one to jump overboard when the ship was sinking. Her first reaction to his announcement was a feeling of betrayal. It must have shown in her face because his next words were defensive.

"I know how you feel, Claire," he began. "But this doesn't have anything to do with the *Voice* business. My ultimate goal has always been to work for a paper with a national standing. But I wouldn't have gone with them now if Sid Golden hadn't contacted me with an offer that was just too good to pass up."

Claire sighed. Another of Spence's predictions had fulfilled itself. And at the worst possible time. He had told her that a one-horse paper couldn't hold its team together forever. She almost smiled at the mixed metaphor. But just now it wasn't in her to be truly amused. As the year slipped away, so, apparently, was the little world she'd built for herself.

Still, she'd brought all this trouble down on her own head. It had nothing to do with Joe. He'd even advised her to take Spence's offer in the first place.

Leaning forward, Claire put a comforting hand on Joe's thin wrist. "It's all right, Joe. Despite everything, I'm really glad for you. I've been lucky to have you this long.

And I've always known that this was going to happen. You're a talented guy, and you deserve a shot at the top."

Her words made him visibly relax. And for the first time since he'd come into the office he smiled. "You're one classy lady, Claire. The time I've spent with you has been a fantastic experience. I won't be leaving the area. In fact, Emerson Mills is so close to Baltimore that there's no reason for me to give up my apartment. I'd like to keep in touch and offer whatever help I can."

"I appreciate that offer," Claire assured him, knowing that she wouldn't be taking him up on it. Joe would have enough to worry about learning the ropes down at the *Sun*. He didn't need her problems too. Nevertheless, she did want to make their parting as amiable as possible.

"To show you there are no hard feelings, let me buy you a drink down at Ethan's," she offered, giving him her warmest smile.

Joe agreed readily. "I'll let you buy the drinks, if you let me take you to dinner, and not at Ethan's. Let's do something more elegant. I've got my reputation to think of now, and being seen with a woman as beautiful as you will do it good."

Claire had laughingly protested. But in the end she'd been persuaded to take Joe up on his offer.

"Why don't we invade enemy territory," he suggested with a wink. "I'll make reservations at Claude's." He named a plush and trendy restaurant in the Newton downtown plaza.

"You mean you're going to spend your whole last week's salary on giving your boss the kiss off?" Claire quipped, keeping her voice light so that Joe wouldn't misinterpret the intent of her words. But despite her precautions, Joe's neck went red with embarrassment anyway.

"It's not a kiss off," he assured her earnestly. "It's a thank you—a very heartfelt and sincere one. I owe you a lot, and I want you to know that I'm grateful."

Claire did know it, and to show Joe that there were no hard feelings she dressed with flair for their friendly "date," choosing a green velvet dress with a full skirt and deep V neckline. The brilliant color made her dark hair shine and brought out the blue of her eyes. Completing her deliberately upbeat color scheme were silver sandals and a matching clutch bag.

"Wow," Joe exclaimed when he caught sight of her. "If you dressed like this at the office, we'd never get the paper out!"

Claire grinned. "Actually, I'm glad you gave me the excuse to get dressed up."

"You're too conservative," Joe scolded as he set his small car in the direction of Newton. "A woman with your looks ought to use every excuse to show off what she's got."

Joe's flattery helped to lighten her mood. By the time they pulled up in the restaurant's elegant circular drive, she had vowed to do her utmost to put aside her cares and enjoy this outing. She knew this was a special occasion for Joe. Claude's was an expensive place, and what he earned at the *Gazette* wouldn't pay for many evenings in such surroundings. She wanted him to enjoy himself.

Furnished with the brass fixtures, stained glass, and heavy oak of a bygone era, Claude's was as well known for its gourmet fare as for its elegant Victorian atmosphere. It was extremely popular with the young professionals in the new city. And even on a Tuesday evening every table was full, and the air was alive with laughter and sophisticated chatter. Despite Joe's reservation, they were ushered into the bar to wait.

"That's what I get for wanting to show off." He shrugged ruefully.

"It doesn't matter," Claire assured him, glancing around at the hanging ferns and enormous polished bar with its heavy brass rail. "I can buy you your drink here just as well as at the table."

They had been sipping their martinis and chatting idly for about ten minutes when something made Claire glance up. Another couple was being ushered into the bar. And when Claire recognized the broad-shouldered male figure, her hand froze on the narrow stem of her cocktail glass. It was Spence McCabe—with Joyce Rushing in tow.

"What is it?" Joe questioned, responding to the suddenly petrification of Claire's features. And then the two figures swung into his line of vision. "Oh, I see," he muttered under his breath. "When I suggested a foray into enemy territory I didn't have anything quite this literal in mind. But I feel up to facing them if you do. Want to ask them to have a drink with us?"

Claire shook her head emphatically. "I don't feel up to that," she whispered hoarsely. "Let's ask the waiter if our table's ready."

Joe shot her a troubled look. He knew only of her business rivalry with Spence, not of their shattered personal relationship.

Claire felt her stomach knot as the couple approached. Fumbling to gather up her purse, she hoped desperately that Spence wouldn't notice her presence at the end of the bar. But that was too much to ask.

As Joe took her elbow and guided her toward the exit,

they were halted by Joyce's cheerful greeting. "Where have you been, Joe? We've missed you at Ethan's lately."

The salutation forced them to stop. And Claire found herself face to face with the last man she had wanted to confront that evening. He was looking remarkably handsome, she couldn't help noticing, in an expensively tailored dark wool suit, subtly striped shirt, and deep ruby silk tie. For a moment their eyes met and locked. And then Claire looked quickly down at the half-finished drink still clutched in her suddenly ice-cold hand.

The warmth she had once basked in was gone from his expression now. And she watched as he took Joyce's arm possessively in his hand.

"How are things going?" he rumbled politely, as though they were simply two casual acquaintances meeting on the street.

"Fine," Claire lied. Things were far from fine and he knew it. But this was hardly the time or place to go into that.

Spence's answer was a noncommittal "Um" before he turned his attention back to Joyce.

Mercifully, Joyce was far more interested in her companion than a long conversation with business acquaintances. After a few more forced pleasantries, Claire and Joe were able to escape. And, fortunately, it was only a few minutes later that the waiter told them their table was ready.

"Well, I guess good old Joyce finally got her wish," Joe ventured after they were seated.

Claire lifted questioning blue eyes to his happy face.

"She had her fishing line out for McCabe months ago. And now it looks like she's finally starting to reel him in," he elaborated with a chuckle.

Claire felt her throat close. Her mind was a total blank. She couldn't think of any reply that would make sense to Joe. And so instead of answering she opened the menu and pretended to be engrossed in its tempting descriptions of expensive dishes she now had absolutely no interest in eating.

Somehow she managed to get through the rest of the evening, only catching sight of Spence and Joyce one other time as they were led to a secluded table in an adjoining dining room. But though Claire tried not to spoil Joe's evening, his expensive treat was wasted on her. The food might have been sawdust. And she had to force herself to down her share of the costly bottle of Bordeaux that he insisted on ordering with a flourish.

"I know this newspaper situation is upsetting you," Joe remarked as he dropped her off later that evening. "But maybe it's not as bad as it seems. I don't think McCabe really wants to destroy the *Gazette*. I think he's just trying to persuade you to agree to his original proposition." Joe turned toward her in the front seat of his car and gave her a searching look. "I know how you feel about selling a controlling interest. But, Claire, let me give you some advice—just as a friend, not as an employee. I think if you want the *Gazette* to survive, you're going to have to reconsider his offer. What's more, I think in the long run it may really be to everyone's benefit. Think about it."

Claire nodded. "I don't know. Maybe you're right. And even if you aren't, I may not have any other choice."

It was too chilly to sit long in the car. And though she offered Joe a cup of coffee, he sensed her withdrawn mood and refused.

Alone in her house at last, she had nothing to distract

her from thoughts of Spence McCabe. She trudged up to her bedroom with leaden steps and began taking off the brilliant green velvet dress that was so at odds with her mood. She had hoped Spence was through hurting her on a personal level. But tonight, seeing him with another woman had been like getting hit by a truck. The blow had been so devastating that she was still feeling the pain.

And yet why should she have been so shocked? she asked herself bleakly. Spence was a healthy, virile man. He had told her that he had finally gotten over the loss of Kathleen and was now capable of loving another woman. Claire could have been that woman, except for her self-centered pride and fear. But now he was lost to her, and she had only herself to blame.

Claire struggled to retain her usual composure, but tonight the overwhelming pain of her loss was suddenly too much. Unconsciously her fingers stroked the soft velvet material still clutched in her hand, as if the simple act could bring her comfort. But when her fingers encountered a spot of wetness on the dress, she quickly put the garment down on the bed and wiped her damp cheek with the back of her hand. *Stop crying,* she told herself sternly. But that was impossible. The first teardrops were only the beginning of a flood. Claire hadn't cried herself to sleep since she'd been a child. But now she threw herself on the bed without bothering to finish undressing and abandoned her pride to the deep misery that had been building inside her for the past weeks.

Although her eyes were swollen in the morning, she did feel somewhat better for the release she'd allowed herself. And as she sipped a cup of coffee in the kitchen, she was able to think about Spence and her situation with him more calmly. She would have to accept the fact that things were over between them. They would never again be lovers. But there were still their business dealings to consider. Spence wanted the *Gazette*. And it looked as if—one way or another—he was going to get it. How much longer could she hold out against his onslaught? she asked herself. And what would happen if she did? It was time to put her personal feelings aside and face cold, hard facts. If she tried to hold out, she'd have to let her staff go. And how could she, in good conscience, turn people out of work just to satisfy her desire to stand fast for a few more months or weeks?

And then there was the problem of replacing her editor. With the salary she'd been able to offer, she'd been very lucky to attract someone like Joe in the first place. But now, with even less financial room to maneuver, there was no way to hire a worthy replacement. What's more, allowing the quality of the paper to slip would be worse in her eyes than selling out.

As she sat sipping her coffee, all of these thoughts tumbled around in Claire's mind like rocks in a washer. She was going to have to come to some decision. And the sooner the better. Sighing, she finally put her coffee cup down.

When Spence had told her that sentimentality and business didn't mix, she hadn't wanted to believe him. But he'd amply demonstrated his point and now it was her move.

Unfortunately, there was nowhere to move. Like a master chess player, Spence had put her in check weeks ago. This was checkmate. The only thing left was to find out if his terms of surrender had changed. And maybe, if she made the overture now, she could get a better deal for her employees and the *Gazette*.

The decision made, Claire went back upstairs to wash her eyes with cold water and repair as much of the night's damage as possible. An hour later she sat before the phone in her office, a hand poised to make the call she'd been dreading for so long. Forcing herself to keep from shaking, she finally reached out and lifted the receiver.

But like so many situations we imagine, the reality was much less traumatic than what she'd built in her imagination.

Spence accepted her capitulation calmly. And he made no attempt to increase the pain of her defeat. Though she'd been prepared to accept much less favorable terms, the deal he offered was the same one he'd originally proposed.

Claire could stay on as publisher of the *Gazette,* only now Spence's corporation would hold the controlling interest in her paper. Day-to-day editorial decisions would still go through her office, but major policy would be set at weekly staff meetings of the two papers.

"I'll have my lawyer send over the papers by the end of the week," Spence finished in a businesslike voice. "You can take the weekend to look them over. And we'll try and get them signed by Tuesday or Wednesday."

As she hung up, Claire already felt like an employee of SJM. In fact, from his dispassionate tone as he restated his terms, it was hard to imagine that she had ever been anything more to the man than a business rival to be swept out of the way.

That he had once proposed marriage to her seemed like a fantasy she had daydreamed. And yet the hours she had spent in his arms were no daydream. They could not have been something she simply imagined.

Stop thinking about that, Claire warned herself. *He*

doesn't want you anymore. And yet she couldn't stop herself from kindling a little glimmer of hope somewhere in the recesses of her mind. She was going to be seeing more of Spence, after all, she told herself. Maybe the close proximity would make a difference.

Resolutely she composed her features. She would have to tell her staff of her decision. And a long face would not set the tone she hoped her words would convey. The *Gazette* was going to go on, albeit in slightly altered form. But the important thing was that it would survive. Summoning all the sense of purpose she could muster, Claire got up from her desk and opened the office door. It remained only to call her staff together and tell them what lay ahead.

CHAPTER ELEVEN

The change of command at the *Gazette* was not accomplished until the first of February. And yet Claire was able to assure her staff that they would not face a new year wondering about their paychecks.

Even before the deal was consummated, morale was definitely on the upswing. And after the papers were signed, the benefits of the merger began to show themselves quickly. Spence included the *Gazette* in his advertising package, so that even during the usually slow period at the end of winter, revenues began to increase.

But Claire quickly learned that the new corporation did not expect to put the paper on a strictly "pay-as-you-go basis."

"We're a team now," Spence told the *Gazette* and *Voice* senior staff at the first joint strategy meeting. "We're not going to be fighting each other anymore. We're going to share the profits and the losses. Our editorial talent will be pooled, with stories used in either or both papers where appropriate. And ad revenues will also be going into a common pot so that whoever needs funds will get them."

Claire couldn't help admiring the forceful manner in which he took charge and the way he inspired the staff. Everyone from the *Gazette* including Claire left the meeting with a hopeful feeling about the paper's future. Spence had even given her carte blanche to find a top new editor at a more than competitive salary.

And yet the meeting left her depressed. If she had entertained any illusions that Spence would warm to her now that he had accomplished his goal, they were sadly dashed by his behavior at the meeting. He had treated her in exactly the same calm, courteous fashion he had shown all the other senior members of her staff. Nothing less—and nothing more.

And that set the tone of their new relationship. She had expected to see Spence frequently, but he apparently wanted to keep their personal contact to a minimum. They seemed to run into each other only at well-attended staff meetings. And when the president of SJM Communications had some message for her, he usually wrote a memo or had his secretary phone.

In a way, she was grateful. Although she loved Spence and longed to be closer to him, she didn't know what she might do if they found themselves unaccompanied. When others were present, the bounds of propriety restrained her. But, alone with him, would she be able to keep from reaching out a hand to touch his shoulder? Or worse, would she be able to keep from blurting some entreaty that she would instantly regret? He had made his personal feelings about her abundantly clear on that terrible day he had come to her house. There was nothing she could say to sway him now. All she could do was embarrass him—and hurt herself.

Claire's only consolation—and it was bitter comfort—was that Joyce Rushing had apparently not replaced her after all. Office scuttlebutt had it that Spence was playing the field now. And his female companions seemed to change frequently.

Maybe I was wrong about him, Claire tried to tell herself. *Maybe he wasn't ready to settle down.*

In a way, the thought made her own situation a little easier to live with. Maybe she hadn't let Spence slip through her fingers because he'd never really been hers in the first place. Deep down, she knew she didn't really believe the rationalization. But it was something to cling to.

Certainly she had made a lot of wrong assumptions in the past. Because she had seen the damage done to other small papers taken over by chains, she had assumed the same thing would happen to the *Gazette*. But now it was clear that Spence's intentions toward her paper had been strictly honorable—just as he'd said they were. The *Gazette* was stronger now as a community organ than it had ever been. There was more coverage of local events and a stronger editorial base because of the increased joint circulation with the *Voice*. Claire could see now that Emerson Mills and Newton had a lot of concerns in common, and that joining the two papers made the *Gazette* twice as effective in influencing county opinion.

As the winter wore on, Claire found herself returning to her old pattern of casual dating. But these evenings out were neither frequent nor prolonged. There was only one man who really interested her. And he was no longer available. So she found that outside of office hours, she was keeping more and more to herself.

But as she ate her lonely dinners and spent her evenings going over press releases, checking feature stories, and writing editorials, she was hard put to find much satisfaction in her life. She had had a brief taste of something else.

And she knew now that this solitary existence, focused on a job that could be done as well by others, was not what she wanted.

Now that the *Gazette* was under such capable management, she mused, maybe she should consider severing her ties. Living this close to Spence was a torment. He was the man she loved. Maybe he wasn't dating seriously now, but eventually he would find someone he could fall in love with. And she didn't want to be around when that happened. Maybe she should go back to New York and start all over, away from the scene of what had been for her a personal disaster of her own making.

And yet, since she had made no real decisions, she was obliged to put up a front of—if not contentment—at least satisfaction.

When Spence insisted that the senior editorial offices be redecorated to give the *Gazette* the prosperous look he wanted to convey, she forced herself to pretend enthusiasm. How ironic, she thought as she sat with the decorator he had engaged, fingering swatches of fabric and wallpaper and matching them to carpet samples. She was being given the opportunity to design her dream office. But now it didn't seem to matter anymore. Chances were she wouldn't occupy it for long.

Nevertheless, the results were a small satisfaction. The old, high-ceilinged room with its natural brick walls and working fireplace was easy to turn into a special hideaway. The addition of thick rose carpeting, muted draperies, and textured wallpaper, together with the antique desk and comfortable lounge chairs she found on Main Street, gave the sunny corner office the look she'd always wanted but could never before afford.

The room became a retreat. More and more often Claire

began closing the door and making herself less accessible to staff members. She even had a small refrigerator installed, which she stocked with exotic cheeses, Perrier, and fruit for lunch.

Was she trying to see if Spence McCabe and her new editors, Tim Glenwood and Sandy Dumont, could run things just as well without her? she asked herself. But she didn't answer the question. She wasn't ready to face the issue yet.

Before Claire realized it, the winter was over. At the end of April the weather turned warm, reawakening the first yellow and purple crocuses in Emerson Mills's gardens and bringing residents who had been huddling indoors for warmth out onto the streets. It was a time of new beginnings. And soon Claire would have to make some sort of decision about her future. But she didn't feel capable of forcing a decision yet. She couldn't bear being so near to Spence McCabe and yet just a business associate. But at the same time, she still couldn't bear to be away from him either.

However, one Friday evening as she washed her dinner dishes and listened to her favorite classical music station, she had an opportunity to find out that she still cared a great deal about the *Gazette*—despite her ambivalence about staying on as publisher.

After the warm spell the weather had turned cold and rainy. And Claire had been glad to change into a warm dressing gown after work and eat before a roaring fire. It seemed like a night for turning in early. And so she tidied the kitchen and washed up quickly. She was just setting her teacup in the drainer, when an announcer broke into the middle of the Brahms symphony she had been enjoying.

* * *

Local flood warnings have been put into effect for all communities south of Baltimore. Residents in low-lying areas near the Patuxent, Pawkata, and Patapsco rivers are particularly advised to evacuate to high ground. Please stay tuned to this station for further bulletins.

Melodious symphonic strains once again filled the kitchen. But Claire was no longer listening. The *Gazette* occupied an old factory building directly on the Pawkata. And in the basement were all those priceless files she had never gotten around to moving. In them were the only copies of some of her father's editorials. If the water flooded the building, they would be destroyed.

There was no thought of personal danger. Claire had to get as many of those old records to the upper floors as she could. But she wasn't going to put anyone else in jeopardy either.

After hurrying up the stairs two at a time, she quickly stepped out of her dressing gown and pulled on a heavy sweat shirt, faded jeans, wool socks, and loafers.

So great was her haste to get down to the *Gazette* that she almost left the house without telling anyone where she was going. But at the last moment she forced herself to pick up the phone and call Tim Glenwood, her new second in command. After all, there was no reason to be foolish about this.

"Want me to meet you there?" he asked.

But Claire could tell from his voice that he would much rather stay warm and dry at home.

"No need for that," she reassured him. "The water probably won't reach the building anyway."

Tim let his mind be set at rest. He'd only been at the *Gazette* a few months, and he had no strong feeling of loyalty to the venerable old paper—and certainly not to a bunch of antique files. But Claire did. And she wasn't going to take any chances.

Pulling on a rain slicker, she dashed for her car. Through the windshield, water was coming down in great, gusty sheets, making visibility almost zero on Main Street. There was no way that Claire could hurry.

When she reached the bridge at the bottom of the hill, she was stopped by a police car.

"Oh, it's you, Miss Tanager," the officer in charge noted as she obediently rolled down her window. "We're getting ready to close the bridge."

"Listen, Roy, I have urgent business at the paper," she appealed. "Can't you let one more car through."

"Well . . ."

"Please. I must get across."

"Well, seeing as it's you. But the water is pretty high. Sure you don't want to just go back home and hole up till this is over?"

Claire shook her head decisively. And Roy let her pass.

Claire stopped in the *Gazette*'s foyer to take off her wet slicker and consider her plan of action.

She had no illusions about how many stacks of old records she could carry up from the storage rooms. They were long corridors away from the stairs and it would take a Hercules to empty them all. But that wouldn't be necessary. Since the *Gazette* building had been converted from an old flour mill rich in eighteenth-century red-brick charm, it also boasted a huge freight elevator—which was almost next to the file room. All she had to do was transfer boxes to the elevator and then bring it up to the second floor.

But the ancient piece of equipment had hardly been used since the *Gazette*'s printing operation moved to Newton. Suppose it was not working? The last time it had been used was months ago, when the new furniture was transported to her office.

Quickly Claire checked out the rickety elevator, breathing a sigh of relief when it proved to be in working order. *I might as well ride it down to the basement,* she told herself, pressing the button.

The heavy door closed and the machinery shuddered to life. With a creak the car started to descend. And then abruptly it stopped. At the same time, the overhead light went out, and Claire was plunged into complete darkness.

She felt panic rising in her chest. What had happened? But the answer was all too abundantly clear. The storm had taken the power lines out.

Calm down, she told herself. *You're not hurt. You're okay.*

But she was alone in the dark like an animal caught in a trap. And she was frightened.

Sinking to the tile floor of the car, she pulled her knees up and clasped them with her arms. Claire had never liked the dark. And she had never liked to be closed in.

Now it took all her willpower to keep from screaming.

Oh, go ahead, if you want to, one part of her brain urged. *Nobody's going to hear anyway.* But that observation was far from comforting. How long was she going to have to stay here? And what would happen if the water really did rise to this level?

And then she remembered, this was a Friday evening. Probably no one would be coming into the building until

Monday morning. Maybe Tim Glenwood would miss her and send someone, she tried to tell herself. But it was hard to put much conviction into the thought.

It took all of Claire's willpower to keep her spiraling fear under control. But she forced herself to make the effort. She wasn't sure what would happen if she let her rising terror get the better of her. And she didn't want to find out.

Pulling herself tighter into a protective ball, she closed her eyes against the pitch darkness. There was not a sound to be heard except the lapping of water below her. Was it coming closer? she wondered.

As her ears strained to find out, she suddenly became conscious of another sound. Footsteps.

There was someone else in the building! Her first impulse was to call out wildly. But she stopped herself. No one was supposed to be here. Maybe someone was taking advantage of the storm to loot the newspaper office.

Shrinking back into the corner, she huddled in fright, listening to the steps come closer and then recede.

And then, from down in the basement, someone was shouting her name.

Instantly she recognized the deep voice vibrating through the building. It was Spence. It couldn't be possible, but it was. He had come looking for her. And her heart leaped at the knowledge.

"Here—I'm in here," she called back, unable to keep the trembling emotion out of her voice.

"Thank God! Where is 'here' "?

"In the elevator. I got stuck when the electricity cut off."

She heard his answering string of expletives. "What are you doing in there?" he questioned, his voice a mixture of incredulity and irritation now. But he didn't wait for her answer. "Never mind. I'm sure it's a long story. But don't you realize that if Tim Glenwood hadn't called me, you could have been stuck here all weekend? Stupidest thing I ever heard of—risking your life for a bunch of files."

Claire knew her actions had been ill considered. She just wished Spence wouldn't rub it in. But before she could frame a defensive answer, he barked another question. "What floors are you between?"

"The first and the basement," she answered promptly. But her gladness at his arrival was tempered now. When he had first heard her voice, she thought she had detected real concern in his answer. But she must have been mistaken.

"Well, hold tight. I'm going up above you then," he replied, all business now.

Claire heard his heavy footsteps pounding up the stairs. And then his voice was above her. "You're lucky; the car is barely below floor level here, and the outside door didn't close. Getting you up here shouldn't be too much of a problem."

In a moment there was a thud directly overhead and the sound of rusty metal giving. Then she was shading her eyes from a flashlight beam flooding in above her head.

"Are you okay?" Spence questioned tensely.

"Yes. Spence, how high is the water?"

"Not high enough to hurt the damn files or drown us," he said in an exasperated tone. "Well, stand out of the way. I'm coming down."

Obediently, Claire moved aside. "I'm going to set down my light," Spence warned before swinging down from the trap door in the ceiling. In a moment he stood beside her.

It had been a long time since she had been this close to

Spence McCabe. And now they were not only close but alone in the semi-darkness. Suddenly, Claire was powerfully aware of his considerable physical presence. Over the past few months she had seen him only dressed for business. But now he wore a pair of faded jeans and a dark turtleneck that clung to his body in a way no business suit could.

"Why—why did you leave your flashlight up there?" Claire stammered, trying to turn her mind to something besides the intimate closeness she was suddenly feeling.

"I'm going to need my hands free to get you out of here," he clipped out, his tone as impersonal as if they were discussing a feature story for the *Gazette*.

"Oh."

"If you get on my shoulders, I can lift you up to the trap door," he explained.

"On your shoulders?" she repeated stupidly. She had hoped to avoid that sort of physical contact. But he was right, of course. How else was he going to get her out of there?

"Yes." As he spoke he knelt below the trap door.

When Claire made no move in response, he looked up at her in exasperation. "I said, climb on my shoulders. We don't have all night."

Gingerly she reached out and touched his back, all too aware of the broad expanse of muscle and sinew beneath the knit material of his shirt. And then, lower lip between her teeth, she forced herself to grasp his shoulders firmly. The action pulled her breasts against his back and she tried to pretend that she was simply standing against a boulder. But it was no good. She could feel the warmth of his body and the yielding firmness of his skin all too well. Desperately she tried to will herself not to react. But there was no way she could stop her nipples from hardening at the intimate pressure.

"I'll steady your legs, and you push yourself up," Spence rumbled gruffly.

Claire felt strong arms reach around to grasp her calves, and then she was being pushed up and forward, her torso against the back of his neck now. "Grab for the edge of the trap door," he directed, and Claire tried to obey. But she was too stiff from sitting in the same position for so long and too aware of the sensations the physical contact with Spence was producing. As he lifted her aloft, her fingers brushed the edge of the trap door opening. But she was unable to grab it fast. Instead, she swayed to the left and Spence had to lower her quickly down his back again to keep her from falling against the wall.

She could hear him cursing softly under his breath. "All right, that's not going to work," she heard him rasp finally. "Let's try something else."

Claire waited tensely for his next move. In the dim light she could see the rigid line of his jaw and his eyes dark and angry.

"Turn around and face me," he ordered, snapping out the command like a karate instructor with a hopeless pupil.

Lowering her head so that she would not have to meet his eyes or feel the caress of his warm breath on her face, Claire complied. She felt his hands grip her waist then. She ached to throw her arms around his neck and pull the length of his body close to her. But that was obviously out of the question. Their closeness might be driving her insane. But all Spence wanted was to get her out of there.

"I'm going to lift you straight up," he growled. "Are you ready?"

Her body stiffened as she felt him begin to thrust her aloft. But he hadn't counted on the loose sweat shirt she was wearing. Instead of staying at her waist, it rode up her torso with his hands. Claire felt cold air on her midriff and tried to twist away. But Spence was too intent on his rescue mission to realize what was happening. "Hold still," he clipped out as he raised her toward the opening. "What in the hell are you trying to do?

Wanting desperately to cooperate, Claire held herself stiffly, knowing that in a few moments her unencumbered breasts would be in Spence's face. But before that quite happened, she felt her upward progress stop.

"My God, Claire," he groaned, "I can't take any more of this."

She heard the fervor in his voice. And there was no way she could stop herself from responding. Bending slightly, she clasped the only part of him that she could reach—his head—against her chest.

Of their own accord her fingers began to stroke the luxuriant thickness of his dark locks. And at the same time she bent to press her cheek against the top of his hair.

"Now, what the hell are you doing," he rasped. "Trying to drive me crazy?"

The words she had held back for so long came unbidden from her lips. "Spence, I love you."

She felt his arms stiffen. "Why are you saying that? Is it just because you're so glad to be rescued?" he asked harshly.

The uncaring words brought hot tears to the backs of her eyes. "All right, you arrogant bastard," she found herself blurting out, her voice thick with emotion, "I didn't mean to say it. Forget it. It's not true."

She didn't know what reaction she expected. But there

was no way she could have anticipated his next action. Slowly he began to lower her until her feet were just touching the floor. But he did not let go of her or thrust her away. Instead, he pulled her tightly up against his body, his massive arms enfolding her like bands of iron. And for the first time she became aware that his attempts to lift her out of the elevator had aroused him as much as they had her.

For a long moment he simply clung to her. And then she felt him bend so that his cheek could press against hers. "Did you mean it?" he questioned softly. And Claire could hear the catch in his voice as he framed the question.

"Yes," she breathed.

"Oh, God, Claire, say it again."

Tenderly, she repeated the words. "I love you, Spence, and I think I've been in love with you since that very first time we were together. But first I was too blind to see it, and then I was too proud to admit it."

If it was possible, he pulled her even closer against his hard frame. But now that she had begun, she couldn't stop more words of contrition from tumbling out. "Oh, Spence, I've been so stupid—and I've made so many mistakes. If I'd just trusted and believed in you the way my heart told me to. Can you ever forgive me for all those stupid things I said to you? I didn't really mean them—it was just my fear and my pride talking."

She felt his hands then moving up under her sweat shirt to caress and stroke the length of her back.

"Claire, I'd forgive you anything. I've loved you from that first night too. When you were gone that morning, all I could think of was how to get you back."

While he talked, his hands had continued to caress her. And she began to ache to have those blunt fingers move around to her breasts. But she knew that if he touched her in that way, all the passion she had been trying to hold in check might explode out of control.

"Claire, it's been torture without you. When I found you, I felt as if I'd been reborn. When you rejected me, it was like being cast back into hell. And these last months I began to doubt I'd ever climb out again. Just being around you and not being able to touch you was torment."

The words were only a confirmation of what his actions had already told her.

"Oh, Spence," she choked out, so overcome with emotion that she could hardly speak.

"And, God, do I want you," he added. "I want to tear you clothes off and make love to you. But not on the cold floor of this damn elevator."

"It doesn't have to be on the floor," Claire found herself saying.

But Spence's answer was a rueful chuckle. "Claire, I'm a good six inches taller than you are. It would never work."

He was right of course. And she found herself grinning at the image his words created.

"So I suggest we get our act together for another escape attempt. Or do you still lack sufficient motivation?"

Claire shook her head. "You've provided the motivation," she admitted.

"And shall we try it from the front or the back this time?" Spence inquired innocently.

"Oh, from the front, by all means," Claire suggested.

"Then tuck your damn sweat shirt in," Spence ordered. "Or I won't be responsible for what happens."

Claire obeyed and then turned to face him. This time, before he grasped her waist, his lips descended to claim hers. She found her mouth opening eagerly to the possessive thrust of his tongue, trying to drink in the essence of this man she loved so much and had thought she had lost forever.

"There are so many things I have to say to you," she managed when the kiss finally ended.

"Me too," he agreed. "But we'll save the rest of it for later. Now that I know I have you back, nothing matters but being as close to you as it's possible to get."

With that he grasped her by the waist again and thrust her upward. This time Claire was able to grab the edge of the trap door opening. And with a boost from Spence, she pulled herself up and through.

For Spence it was only a matter of jumping upward and grabbing the edge of the opening. In a moment he, too, had swung his body up and gained the top of the elevator.

It was only an easy step up to the first floor. The driving rain had stopped and there was moonlight coming in from the high windows along the hallway and stairwell. Spence reached down to switch off the flashlight.

"Well?" he inquired, turning toward Claire. "You know this building better than I do. Where would you suggest we go?"

While she considered the question, she felt Spence's hand begin to stroke the back of her neck and then reach up to tangle suggestively in her dark hair.

"You're not exactly making it easy for me to think," she murmured just before he turned her body once more toward his and took her lips in a hot, demanding kiss that left no doubt about his intentions.

"Maybe my office," she managed when his lips had left hers to trail tantalizing little kisses along the line of her jaw and then down to the sensitive spot where her neck and shoulders joined.

He was unable to keep his hands off her now. She felt them loosen her sweat shirt again and steal inside before moving hungrily upward.

When they reached her breasts, Claire drew in her breath sharply. The pleasure was as piercingly intense as she had anticipated. Her nipples hardened to little knots of eager sensation. And when Spence pulled up the loose shirt so that his mouth and lips could continue the caress his hands had begun, she felt her knees buckle as her whole body seemed to melt with overwhelming desire.

"Spence," she whispered, "I'll never make it upstairs under my own power."

In answer he swung her up into his arms, carrying her easily up the broad, dimly lit stairs.

When they gained her office, Spence set her gently down on her feet. "I wish you'd ordered a nice wide bed when you had this place redecorated," he commented, glancing around the shadowy room.

Outside in the moonlight the river rushed past, far above its banks. But neither of them paid it any heed.

"We made love on the rug that first time, didn't we?" Claire reminded him. "I guess it will do as well again."

"Yes," he agreed. And Claire could hear the passion in his voice. "And much as I'm confident of my ability to warm you, I think I'd better light us a fire again."

Wood and kindling were in the basket next to the fireplace. Spence set quickly about putting them to good use. Unable to separate herself even briefly from the man she loved, Claire knelt beside him on the rug, her hand stroking his shoulders and back possessively as he worked.

Ordinarily, Spence would have waited to see if the logs

blazed up. But tonight he was too impatient. Turning impetuously to Claire, he pulled her into his arms again and lowered her gently to the thick carpet. Lying down beside this man was a luxury Claire had thought she would never experience again. But now that he held her close once more, her joy was boundless. Quickly she disengaged herself so that she could tug the sweat shirt over her head.

Spence swiftly followed suit and then pulled her tightly against his hair-rough chest. "So good," he murmured. "So good to feel your breasts against me again."

Her answer was a moan of pleasure. But that sweet intimacy was very soon not nearly enough.

"Let me get the rest of my things off," she whispered urgently. And Spence was glad to yield to her request.

She felt his hands reach for her body, stroking in wonder from shoulder to thigh. Then his fingers and lips began to caress her in all the ways he knew would bring delight.

"Ah, Spence . . ." She almost sobbed his name, so intense was the bliss he could create.

Her breath was ragged now. And without conscious thought her hands went to the buckle of his belt so that she could dispatch the last barrier that separated their flesh.

When it was accomplished, he pulled her down on top of him, seeking her lips with an urgency that spoke of incalculable longing. He murmured against her lips, "I want to be able to see your body when we make love."

Drawing back slightly, she looked down into his passion-dark eyes. "Now," he urged.

"Yes."

She had only to move upward and then thrust her hips down again to bring him inside her. For a moment she held herself still, marveling again at the way he filled her and savoring the moment of their joining. But when Spence began to stroke the undersides of her breasts and then move toward her hardened nipples, it was impossible to remain still. The months of denial had stoked their common passion to a fever pitch.

"Claire, Claire," Spence murmured as she set the pace of their pleasure. In the flickering firelight, his lovedrugged eyes roamed hungrily over her face and body, caressing her even as his hands fueled her building need for release.

Her movements became wilder and quicker, serving their mutual ecstasy, spiraling upward to a plane of pure rapture that seemed impossible. For a moment out of time it was as though they were one being, joined by a primal force beyond their separate destinies. She heard him cry out as he shuddered convulsively beneath her. And then she, too, was lost in that explosion of pure sensation she could share only with Spence.

When it was over, he pulled her down beside him, enfolding her in his strong arms and holding her tight against the span of his body. "Unless you've got a cache of blankets hidden around here, I think we're going to be glad of that fire now," he rumbled.

"Um," she murmured sleepily.

Spence moved one arm so he could see his watch. "No wonder you're tired. It's after two in the morning. And then, too, I've been making you do all the work."

She giggled. "Not all. I'd say you had a, er, hand in it."

She felt rather than saw his answering grin of satisfaction.

It was a long time that they lay in each other's arms

then, enjoying the closeness they both had craved so much. But even with the fire and the warmth of Spence's body, Claire found that she was beginning to shiver.

"Wish I could take you home where we'd be more comfortable," Spence observed. "But I barely got in here myself. I don't think the building's really in any danger, but the approaches are flooded."

The flood. Claire had forgotten all about it, although saving her father's files was the reason she had come down here in the first place. She sighed with relief. Spence brushed his lips against her hair. "Much as I'm loath to make the suggestion," he murmured, "I think we need to put our clothes back on. It's just too damn cold in here with the heat off."

Claire had to agree. Quickly they dressed again. And Spence added more wood to the fire. "If we run out, we can always burn old *Voices,*" he quipped. "I'm sure that wouldn't bother you at all."

Claire moved into the circle of his arms again. "I might have felt that way once," she admitted. "But you must know you've changed my mind. You taught me a lot about the newspaper business, things I was too prejudiced to see for myself."

In answer, his lips brushed the top of her head.

She felt so safe and contented in his arms. And yet, there were things—much more personal things—that needed to be said between them.

"Spence," she began tentatively.

"Mmm?"

It was hard to continue. But she forced the words out. "I know how much I hurt you. I've known it for a long time. You were offering me your love, and I rejected you."

Spence looked away. But at the same time his arm tightened around her shoulder.

"Yes, you hurt me," he admitted soberly. "You don't know how damn hard it was for me to commit myself to someone again. And then when you didn't want me . . ."

Not knowing what to say now, Claire pressed her face against his shoulder.

They sat in silence for a moment, and then Spence cleared his throat. "I still wanted you, Claire. God, did I still want you. Nobody else I dated this winter meant a damn thing to me. But I just couldn't be vulnerable to you again—especially after that lunch of yours with Buchanan."

Claire shook her head. "Spence, I swear it was only lunch. And even when I agreed to go I knew how much more you meant to me than he ever did. I knew I wanted you, and I was coming home to tell you—"

But he cut off her explanation. "That was a case of *my* mouth working before my brain had a chance to catch up. I don't think I ever really believed you were having an affair with Buchanan. But you'd hurt me so badly that I wanted to hurt you back. If I just hadn't reacted like a wounded bull elephant, we would have been married at Christmas, not miserable all winter. That afternoon I wanted to wound you too. But after that I knew that if I were alone with you, I'd probably give up and pull you into my arms again."

Spence tightened his arm around her shoulder and brushed his lips tenderly across her cheek. "And that's what I wanted you to do. But I couldn't tell you," Claire admitted.

"I used to drive by your house and look at those damn

lights in your windows and wish I were inside with you," Spence confided. "And late in the evenings I used to come over here and sit in your office. After you redecorated the room, it was sort of like being with you."

She turned and clung to him then, tears of mixed joy and regret for the way they had hurt each other stinging the backs of her eyes.

"Claire," he began, his own voice thick with emotion. "I loved Kathleen very much. But she was my past. You're my future—and I know we have a very special, precious future together."

Claire snuggled closer into the shelter of his arms. "Oh, Spence, I was thinking about going away. I thought you didn't want me anymore."

He tightened his hold and shook his head fiercely. Claire could hear his words reverberating in his chest as he spoke. "I was almost crazy with wanting you. The flood just galvanized me into action. But I couldn't have stood seeing you and not being able to touch you much longer. I would have had to make another try to get you back—no matter what the cost if you rejected me again."

The admission brought tears to Claire's eyes. She had always known that this man was unwavering. But now his vulnerability moved her even more than his strength. He was a man she could cherish and love forever—and know that she always had first place in his heart.

Nothing could erase the months of anguish they had both endured. And yet, the bright future that suddenly stretched before them would make up for it.

Spence pulled Claire tight against his body as he leaned back and brought her down to a prone position on the rug again.

"I know getting dressed was my idea," he admitted

huskily. "But even corporate executives make the wrong decisions occasionally."

Claire found herself grinning happily in return. "Just so you're willing to rectify the mistake," she murmured, her hands already under the knit fabric of his shirt.

"Wait a minute," he commanded. "Before we get too far into this, I want to make a date with you. I know this fabulous honeymoon inn with huge heart-shaped tubs, and mirrored ceilings and—"

Claire cut off his words with a giggle. "Are you making a decent or an indecent proposition?" she questioned.

"Both," he promised, before claiming her lips hungrily with his own.

LOOK FOR NEXT MONTH'S
CANDLELIGHT ECSTASY ROMANCES ®

202 REACH FOR THE STARS, *Sara Jennings*
203 A CHARMING STRATEGY, *Cathie Linz*
204 AFTER THE LOVING, *Samantha Scott*
205 DANCE FOR TWO, *Kit Daley*
206 THE MAN WHO CAME TO STAY, *Margot Prince*
207 BRISTOL'S LAW, *Rose Marie Ferris*
208 PLAY TO WIN, *Shirley Hart*
209 DESIRABLE COMPROMISE, *Suzanne Sherrill*

Journey across 19th century Europe with lovers whose deepest passions are ignited, whose loftiest destinies are fulfilled.

The Heiress Series

Roberta Gellis

- ☐ THE ENGLISH HEIRESS, #1 $2.50
- ☐ THE CORNISH HEIRESS, #2 $3.50
- ☐ THE KENT HEIRESS, #3 $3.50

At your local bookstore or use this handy coupon for ordering:

Dell DELL BOOKS
P.O. BOX 1000, PINE BROOK, N.J. 07058-1000

B042A

Please send me the books I have checked above. I am enclosing $ _____ (please add 75c per copy to cover postage and handling). Send check or money order—no cash or C.O.D.'s. Please allow up to 8 weeks for shipment.

Name _____

Address _____

City _____ State/Zip _____

There are strong women. And then there are legends. Knowing one could change your life.

The Enduring Years

Claire Rayner

Hannah Lazar triumphs over grinding poverty, personal tragedy, and two devastating wars to see the children of her shattered family finally re-united. Making her own fortune in a world that tried to break her heart, she endures to become a legend. $3.95

At your local bookstore or use this handy coupon for ordering:

Dell | **DELL BOOKS** | THE ENDURING YEARS $3.95
P.O. BOX 1000, PINE BROOK, N.J. 07058-1000 | B042B

Please send me the above title. I am enclosing $＿＿＿ (please add 75c per copy to cover postage and handling). Send check or money order—no cash or C.O.D.'s. Please allow up to 8 weeks for shipment.

Mr/Mrs/Miss ＿＿＿＿＿＿＿＿＿＿＿＿＿＿＿＿＿＿＿＿＿＿＿＿＿＿＿＿＿＿＿＿＿

Address ＿＿＿＿＿＿＿＿＿＿＿＿＿＿＿＿＿＿＿＿＿＿＿＿＿＿＿＿＿＿＿＿＿＿＿

City ＿＿＿＿＿＿＿＿＿＿＿＿＿＿＿＿＿＿＿＿＿＿＿＿＿ State/Zip ＿＿＿＿＿＿

Desert Hostage

Diane Dunaway

Behind her is England and her first innocent encounter with love. Before her is a mysterious land of forbidding majesty. Kidnapped, swept across the deserts of Araby, Juliette Barclay sees her past vanish in the endless, shifting sands. Desperate and defiant, she seeks escape only to find harrowing danger, to discover her one hope in the arms of her captor, the Shiek of El Abadan. Fearless and proud, he alone can tame her. She alone can possess his soul. Between them lies the secret that will bind her to him forever, a woman possessed, a slave of love. **$3.95**

At your local bookstore or use this handy coupon for ordering:

Dell

DELL BOOKS DESERT HOSTAGE 11963-4 $3.95
P.O. BOX 1000, PINE BROOK, N.J. 07058-1000 B042C

Please send me the above title. I am enclosing $ _____ (please add 75c per copy to cover postage and handling). Send check or money order—no cash or C.O.D.'s. Please allow up to 8 weeks for shipment.

Name _____

Address _____

City _____ State/Zip _____

Candlelight Ecstasy Romances

BREEZE OFF THE OCEAN by Amii Lorin	$1.75	#22	(10817-9)
RIGHT OF POSSESSION by Jayne Castle	$1.75	#23	(17441-4)
THE CAPTIVE LOVE by Anne N. Reisser	$1.75	#24	(11059-9)
FREEDOM TO LOVE by Sabrina Myles	$1.75	#25	(12530-8)
BARGAIN WITH THE DEVIL by Jayne Castle	$1.75	#26	(10423-8)
GOLDEN FIRE, SILVER ICE by Marisa de Zavala	$1.75	#27	(13197-9)
STAGES OF LOVE by Beverly Sommers	$1.75	#28	(18363-4)
LOVE BEYOND REASON by Rachel Ryan	$1.75	#29	(15062-0)
PROMISES TO KEEP by Valerie Ferris	$1.75	#30	(17159-8)
WEB OF DESIRE by Jean Hager	$1.75	#31	(19434-2)
SENSUOUS BURGUNDY by Bonnie Drake	$1.75	#32	(18427-4)
DECEPTIVE LOVE by Anne N. Reisser	$1.75	#33	(11776-3)

At your local bookstore or use this handy coupon for ordering

Dell **DELL BOOKS**
P.O. BOX 1000, PINEBROOK, N.J. 07058-1000

B042D

Please send me the books I have checked above. I am enclosing $ _____ (please add 75c per copy to cover postage and handling). Send check or money order—no cash or C.O.D.'s. Please allow up to 8 weeks for shipment.

Mr. Mrs. Miss _____

Address _____

City _____ State Zip _____